# HOW THE UNIVERSE DANCED WITH THE SUN AND MOON

Written by: Jawanza Wilson

INSTAGRAM- DST_BLUEJAY

Beams of bright light gleamed through the open window into the dimmed room, emphasizing the silhouette of a fast working man. The colors danced, careless of the temporary changes made to the dark brown canvas, to the beat of random clicks and taps. The man lightly rubbed the tips of his fingers over the thick black hairs along his jaw while his eyes studied the collection of words and pictures on the digital plane. He readjusted himself and relaxed his hands on the keyboard before moving his right hand to scroll through the pages on his monitor. Soon, a soft, high-pitched sound warned him of a change in his environment, and instinctively he turned to witness what was coming.

A woman entered gracefully, balancing a cup by the handle. She hesitated for a moment before she pushed the door with her elbow to make more space between her rounded abdomen and the doorknob.

"Duke, you're going to ruin your eyes acting like this!" she said as her elbow was tasked again; this time, gently brushing against the wall.

A brightened light revealed the hidden beauty in the decorated room. "Hey gorgeous," Duke said softly, dragging the pronunciation of "Hey". He pressed the thicker portion of his palm to soothe his irritated left eye and leaned back in his office chair. The young black woman walked next to him and placed a light blue cup with escaping steam in front of him. At first she faked repulsiveness when he tightened his eyelids and poked out his lips, but then she smiled and leaned in to kiss him.

"Mm," he said, licking his lips friskily. "How are we holding up?" he asked as he pulled her closer to him by her waist.

"We're fine," she replied as she placed her hand on her hip and studied the monitor. "I thought you were finished with this?" she asked, giving him the side eye.

Duke laughed as he tapped her on the butt before leaning closer to the monitor.

"You laughing, yet you do this shit all the time," she said as she placed her index finger on the monitor and scrolled through Duke's documents.

"No, I don't," Duke replied, and dazed off for a second before bringing the ceramic cup to his lips.

"You see my face?" she said, staring down at Duke with a raised eyebrow, but Duke smiled and stared at the screen with the cup balanced on his bottom lip. She then bent down with the same expression until Duke gave in and glanced at her face. "Mmm-hmm, that's what I thought," she said, carefully pushing the side of his head.

"Whatever," Duke replied as he placed the cup down. "I'm done. I just wanted to go over things."

"Okay, but who's replacing you? That should have been priority one."

"You're right, but I have an idea of who I want. Got info on them and everything, but most of them are within the company. So, I just have to... step back," Duke replied, scrolling down to a page full of profile pictures.

"Ooooh, it's gonna be okay," she said, teasing him. "My big baby gonna miss bossing people around."

Duke shook his head.

"Just make sure I don't have two," she said, kissing Duke on the forehead before making her way to the exit.

Duke glanced over his shoulder to gain a perspective of the woman as she walked carelessly to the door. "I'll be there in a minute"

"Uh... huh," she replied, not pausing in her departure.

Duke faced the screen again and scrolled down until his eyes fell upon a script. He took a deep inhale through his nose as he dragged his phone closer to him and placed it securely in his palm. A few moments later, he stared into the frontal camera, constantly adjusting and clearing his throat. Then, he spoke.

"Good morning,

"As some of you may have heard. I will be taking an extended break from the company for personal reasons. A little backstory: Yes, our want has manifested, and I am having a baby. I would like to take a moment to thank everyone for their support and positive advice for my family. I'm aware I was secretive about this situation. But the best way I can explain it is... I was shocked... emotional. My first thought wasn't to tell the world. I felt like I just had to get things perfect, and... although I can see a future, I will never be as prepared as I want to be.

"That being said, I will take advantage of what time I have now and heavily invest in how I can make my family's foundation strong enough to face the fears that I and others have. These are based on my own assumptions, but nevertheless, I believe I should step down from my position. I understand that to those invested in the company, my absence can affect the productivity and efficiency of the company. In response to that, the various departments will be supervised by trusted employees whom you all will get to know on a business level, and I will advise things from a distance.

"I am also looking to invest in representatives for the consistent events and programs my wife and I have been involved in. A detailed description of how the business will operate was typed and emailed to current partners and investors, as well as documents and contact information to handle any wanted changes affecting your financial and/or political stake. The public who have signed up to receive newsletters and promotions will receive a less detailed video outlining the changes to come. As always, I look forward to advancing the future for all descendants of African gods and goddesses. Thank you for your time."

* * *

"Mmm," the young man hummed after he listened to the video, keeping his focus fixated on the suburban territory ahead. As he slowed for the traffic change, his brown eyes impulsively glanced at the rearview mirror until older gentleman in the passenger seat took his attention.

The older man squinted as he glided his finger across the brightened phone screen in silence. "You good, Dad?" the driver asked before he pressed on the gas pedal.

"He also wrote that there's an opportunity in his healthcare branch. I say apply, get your foot in," his father said, without acknowledging the question. "You're going to be right there next to Duke. Plus, he's giving you time to work in the field you keep crying about."

The young man jerked his head back with poked out lips. "I don't cry!" he responded with a little excitement. He paused a second while the passenger snickered like an immature child. "And you said I wasn't the 'crier' in the family... so, ha," the man snapped back.

"I didn't say you never would be," the passenger laughed boastfully as the driver stayed stoic. "But seriously, apply, and we'll see what happens. You say you want to be an engineer, right?"

"Chemical, but yeah, I know what you mean," the young man responded with a soft tone.

The man snapped his fingers in response to the statement. "Right, right. Bottom line, you're not going to get where you want by tiptoeing around things just because it isn't exactly what you want. Build up some credit, and then you'll be there."

The driver nodded in agreement as he turned the wheel and pulled to a stop. The sound of a train vibrated the windows as it passed, but the two men continued unfazed. They weaved through traffic until a pedestrian called for a halt in action.

The older man leaned forward slightly and checked the digital clock. "I still got five minutes," the passenger finally said as they arrived at the train station, leaning back in the chair. "No need to rush."

"Okay."

"But getting back to what I was saying, what do you plan to do?"

The driver shrugged his shoulders. "I put my resume out there and talked to a couple places." His hands shook as he turned the wheels to fit between two vehicles. "Nothing biting yet, but I mean, if anything... I'll probably go back... get better credentials."

His father took a deep breath. "We'll sit down and draw something up." He grasped the driver's broad shoulder and shook. "Pop the trunk."

The driver smiled. "I got you."

A moment later, the man pressed his graying beard against the window and continuously pointed down. "I love you."

The driver fidgeted. "Love you too," he replied.

"Tell your mother I'll be home late. You know I forgot," the man said before tapping the car and walking away with his travel bag glued to his back.

The driver waited until his father disappeared behind the wall that hid the top portion of the escalator occupied with commuters. Then the young man, Josiah, tilted his head and gazed off into the distance as his hands worked to put the car in the proper gear.

"'Ight, Josiah..." he whispered to himself as the car was maneuvered to the first set of traffic lights. He waited patiently for about three seconds before he released the steering wheel and grabbed his phone from the cup holder.

Without worry, he held the phone in clear view and only acted more responsible when his eyes landed on a post that caught his attention. He impatiently scanned the area and then grunted at the sight of the bright red light.

"Mmm..." Josiah mumbled to himself as he read the details under a soundless video. "'All necessities provided with pay'. I'm bouta ask for a milli... shit, that's necessary for peace of mind," Josiah said with a higher pitch, and snickered. He scanned around again just in time to see that the opposite lights had changed to yellow, and jolted a little in his seat. He rushed to drop his phone in the cup holder, but missed, and it bounced off the plastic edge and the passenger seat until it hit the floor.

***

A loud metallic bang attracted the attention of two young men formerly seated comfortably on the purple bleachers. The one nearest the dropped object laughed hysterically under the roar of a captive crowd as they marveled over the athleticism displayed on the organized mats set as an individual stage. The man beside him sighed while he gazed at the black phone case that laid face down at the feet of the amused party. He scratched the curls that trickled down to his twisted face. "James," he said.

"I was already getting it," James said after he picked up the fallen device and swung his locks behind his head while he waited for his friend to take the phone.

"Thanks," the young man said as he reached down to open a black bag centered between his legs. "Thought I could balance it on my leg," he continued with a chuckle as he watched his friend shake his head. Soon, their attention was back on the actions on the padded mats below, until the clumsy man broke character again and found himself immersed in the bright light of the shaky phone screen on his thigh.

"Mayruhk, look at this man. Man, you gonna drop that thing again," James said as he watched Mayruhk shift between exploring his bag and tapping on his phone. "Just hold it."

"I was supposed to be grabbing something, but then I lost track," Mayruhk explained as he covered his phone with one hand. "Damn bro, what was I supposed to do?"

"This man, Mayruhk. How'd you get through college, but you always forgetting something?" his friend teased.

Mayruhk laughed outright and made a small scene. "A lot of cheating. I be like, 'yo, stop playing, a black man gotta reputation out here, where them answers at?'"

"This man..." his friend responded.

Mayruhk pointed his finger at his friend. "But only enough so motherfuckers don't get wise on a black man. Mmmmm... words to think about in your future."

"Man, get outta here with that, we already graduated."

"Yeah, but I ain't gonna lie. I miss it. I know it's not the end-all, be-all, but it was fun doing dumb shit and having fun while it lasted," Mayruhk explained before he focused on his blackened phone screen "Mmm, I just remembered."

"What?"

"I was gonna clean off my mouth guard," Mayruhk answered.

"Mannnn!" James responded while dragging the latter portion of the pronunciation. "They already said your name and everything. You should'a done that a while ago."

"I know," Mayruhk admitted as he took a water bottle and dumped some of the contents on a small towel. He propped his phone on his leg once again as he washed down his mouth guard and continued to read where he left off; using his pinkie finger to occasionally scroll through the page.

"Manning! Mayruhk!" announced a booming voice.

"Ooh, shoot," Mayruhk said to express his excitement. He rushed to place the mess of items in his bag and scrambled to collect his phone and a light blue card. "Hey James, can you watch my shit?" Mayruhk asked, but continued to walk off as if he knew the answer.

James raised his hand as he held focus on a match at the far end of the room.

"Okay, good. Please write your name and then proceed to mat five," the kind woman explained. She smiled and waited for Mayruhk to finish his last pen stroke prior to continuing her verbal instruction with added gestures. "Thank you very much. Just wait to the side, you have space to warm up a little and then you will walk up to the green padded area when the other competitor exits before your match. After that, the referee will be in charge of whether it is safe to proceed onto the mat and begin your match. Do you have any questions right now?"

"No, thank you," Mayruhk answered, his eyes hypnotized by the series of mats, active and inactive competitors, coaches, and game officials. Numbers hovered over each mat, which made it easy to identify placement through the sea of people.

After navigating, he found a place with some distance between the crowd around his destination. He watched the closest match for a moment before he studied his surroundings once more with his hands tightly gripped to his hood.

Shortly after, Mayruhk began shuffling his feet. He moved in any direction with fast shifts and precise angle changes while grabbing the air and tugging viciously during certain techniques. Head movement soon followed, and it soon became evident to people who passed by that this young man had taken the challenge of his imaginary opponent as Mayruhk drilled takedowns and escapes with intensity.

"Mayruhk Manning! Jeffery Alston!" yelled the referee, and he motioned the two men onto the mat, only to raise both hands for each participant to finally point at the green area. Mayruhk quickly tightened his gray belt after stripping the hoodie from underneath his gi.

The official took a quick glance, and then turned to each of his peers for confirmation. He followed this action with a motion, guiding the two men to cross the white line connected to the square around the mat.

Finally, when the competitors lined their bare toes along the lone white strips that separated them; the official displayed two colored flags with Velcro straps at an end of each strip.

The official pointed with a flag in each hand and shouted, "Red! Blue! Now, ya too old for wanting favorite colors, so don't get me started," he chuckled as he placed the flags on the backside of each player prior to a step back and final observations. He slowly raised his hand until his thumb was the highest appendage. "Be safe and remember the rules reviewed beforehand. Thank you for your professional attitude and being well-mannered athletes. Time? *Hajime!*"

As if a gunshot had sounded, the two opponents were immediately in action. They carefully danced around each other. Mayruhk constantly faked grabs and shifted his angles while Jeffery played more defensive with his approach, but occasionally would offset his rhythm with threats of clean takedowns. Mayruhk shook his head as he dipped to the left and reached out to grab the lapel.

Soon Jeffery took the bait; he committed heavily to a *seoi nage* into a *tai otoshi*, but it was quickly evaded. Mayruhk finally began to use his height advantage, and reached over his opponent to grab the gi material at the center of his back.

Jeffery shook his arms and upper body viciously, which forced Mayruhk to constantly refasten his grip. With almost any given opportunity, Jeffery jerked Mayruhk's lapel as he avoided an array of foot placements. The two continued their dance back and forth as they attempted to extract their opponent's will to win through physical dominance.

Finally, Mayruhk reinforced his grip on the meaty part of Jeffery's latissimus dorsi, which caused his opponent to twitch in pain. He took advantage, and performed *uchi mata* with precision and speed.

"*Ippon!*" shouted the referee after the thud when Mayruhk slammed his opponent's back to the mat. Part of the crowd paused their commotion after not being able to process the sound, but Mayruhk was focused on the disappointment on his opponent's face as he raised his hands to cover it.

The referee stood silent for a moment while his eyes changed focus between the officials and the competitors. "Can you stand?" he asked with slight concern in his tone and waited with anticipation for a response. Without warning, Jeffery hopped up and walked proudly to the line tape he'd stood on at the beginning of the match. "Bow," the referee demanded after the two fixed their tattered belts.

* * *

Josiah bent over in his seat after he parked in the strip mall's mostly vacant car lot to reach for his phone, which he had lost track of. "Come on," he said to himself and strained until his hand wrapped around a small rectangular object. "I won," he said as he sat back triumphantly.

He gazed upon the early afternoon parties of shoppers with unorthodox work schedules, gym addicts, and an unusual amount of kids for a mid-September day. Josiah shook his head as he attempted to exit the car. "Oh shit," he mumbled. He rushed to remove his phone from his pocket and followed through with his initial motions. "Ight bet," he said and then shut the driver door.

The name Apollo highlighted the store's bight nature as large lettering ran across he upper portion of its face in different colors. But Josiah wasn't impressed by the common landmarks of his town as he passed through the automated doors and sheepish traffic. As if following the stereotypical male trend associated with shopping, he weaved through the isles of the square shaped department until his arms only carried what was reviewed in his mind.

"Hey, how you doing," Josiah said to the distracted clerk as he placed the items on the convey belt." My fault."

"Excuse me for that," the clerk said after standing up and then rotated his ankle for a bit while he scanned the food with his phone-like device with a square attachment.

"You good," Josiah replied, constantly studying the menu above the clerk's head.

"That's all, my man?" the clerk asked while Josiah focused on everything but him.

"Yes," Josiah responded gently while he searched through his pocket. He raised his phone in clear view of the clerk and waited until the man finished organizing the food before he hovered the phone over the counter. Josiah tapped the man's device on the topmost part and awaited a response.

"Ummm, it ain't go through," the man admitted with a concerned expression.

Josiah squinted his eyes while looking at the ground through the left corner of his eyes. "Mmmm," he said, and proceeded to quickly tap on his phone's screen. "I'm sorry give me a second," Josiah said and then turned to the woman behind him. "Did you want to step up?"

The woman raised her hand only a few inches from where it laid on top of the other arm, as if to shrug.

Josiah sighed. "Okay, thank you," he said while swiping his finger in a pattern of up and down or left to right. "Can you take off one of the orange juice, the Kit Kat, and the cake? She'll just have to be mad at me," Josiah said, followed by a breathy laugh and smile.

"Nah, I feel ya bro," the clerk responded as he typed on the device. "'Ight, lemme tap that one more... pause," the clerk said jokingly.

Josiah shook his head after completing the transaction and getting the 'thumbs up' signal. "Good looks, my man."

"You good, bro. Stay safe out there, you hear?" the clerk said and smiled as he invited the next customer.

Josiah raised his hand in acknowledgment as he pressed his back against the door that gave in to his weight. He instinctively went through his usual motions; open the driver's side door, toss the bags to the passenger side, and get in. At his final step, he hesitated to shut the door while stationed in the driver's seat, drawn to the sight of his recent shopping experience.

With a sharp exhale, he prepared the car for the ride to come, and drowned out the noise of passing transportation, along with people either leaving the strip mall or walking by.

Josiah hung his head as he turned the knob, but soon let his head jump to the heavy bass. He sat for a short while and watched the random occurrences that happened in the surrounding parking lot.

Soon, his attention was captured by an old gray minivan that turned into one of the empty park spaces beside him. "You not deadass," Josiah mumbled to himself as he surveyed empty spaces with no surrounding cars not much further from his spot or the entrance. "Fucking lazy ass goofball son... just straight goofy... damn," he described the woman with vocal intensity and immediately shifted the gear to drive away amongst the kicked up leaves from burnt tires.

\* \* \*

A leaf drifted past the glaring eyes of an elderly woman as she stood menacingly within one of the frames of her cream-colored house. The trees' overcast darkened the grey top to the single family to complete the image the encompassed the motion picture of a woman in a pink gown observing the cracked streets.

"Who you trynna scare, Grandma?" Mayruhk asked, then followed with a soft chuckle as he laid on his stomach with his laptop in front of him.

"I thought I heard somebody out there talking that mess," his grandmother responded as she shuffled toward him and kicked at him with her furry slippers. "I also came to tell you to get off my floor and use the table."

Mayruhk chuckled as gleefully as an innocent-minded child while on the hardwood floor. "Alright," he said to himself as he closed the laptop. Once up, he slid to the dining room table with his socks.

"Boy!" the woman shouted. She paused a moment with her right hand on her hip while tightly holding a rag. "Who the hell told you to... figure skate in my house?" she asked while her hand danced, palm up, throughout the entirety of the statement. "I should slap you upside your head."

How the Universe Danced With the Sun and Moon

Mayruhk smiled. "Come on, Grandma. You know you love me. Why would you do that?"

"I love my house more!" his grandmother responded while she opened the oven door.

Mayruhk giggled like an excited young child. "Okay, okay," he responded and dragged the chair from under the dining room table. He listened for a response to the soft scratching noise, but she didn't turn. Silence blanketed the room for a short while as Mayruhk got comfortable; he opened his laptop and watched as the screen re-uploaded his open tabs.

"Oooh, yeah... um, that company... hang on," Mayruhk burst with excitement and then slowly dimmed down his attitude. "Hudson Financial sent me an email, and they said they want me to come in for an interview. I don't want to take it, though."

"Why's that?" his grandmother asked after she paused her activities.

"I feel like they're going to take me in and then use me as that token black guy to make their brochure look good," Mayruhk admitted. "I'd rather give my skills to a black-owned company, rather than continue to not be comfortable."

"But wait," his grandmother responded with a look of concern, complete with folded arms and angled hips. "That's that company you interned at... right?"

"Yeah."

17

"Did they do something to you?" she asked, moving closer to her grandson.

"Nothing blatant, I think. But... I don't know. I felt off about them, like I was being treated some way. And I guess I was a lot more naïve before, so I just took whatever at the time, but as I got older and got into my studies more... yeah, I started noticing certain habits or information I had to find out for myself."

"So, you decided to say something now rather than tell me about it before?" she said with a raised eyebrow. "Send me the name of the company and whomever is important or playing games."

"I'm just not going to go, just in case. So, I can avoid it altogether," Mayruhk pleaded, but was met with a blank stare. "I got you, Grandma."

"Mm-hmm, don't mess with me, boy. You know I don't tolerate the dumb shit Euro-America does." She returned to the stove to stir a steaming silver pot. "You can find another. You're smart, and don't want to settle for deceit and abuse. Trust."

Mayruhk nodded and returned to face his laptop. "But I applied to some black-owned businesses, since ultimately I want to help the community.

"Mmkay, who did you apply to?" his grandmother asked over the sounds of silver dishes hitting the bottom of the sink.

"Uh... gimme a second," Mayruhk replied as he desperately pressed on the touch pad. "Amirnation, and..." Mayruhk paused and let the frantic sounds of keyboard presses fill the void.

"What's wrong?"

"I swore I got emails from like at least three companies, but I... I don't see anything," Mayruhk replied with a growing worry. He paused at moments between frantically searching the screen, until it all stopped. "Yeah... I don't know, but okay, there's at least one I've applied to."

Mayruhk's grandmother inched closer, until she stood beside him and covered the laptop in her shadow. "Find out what happened?"

"No," Mayruhk immediately replied as he shrugged with an open hand. The frustration became clear when the same open hand slammed on the table.

"Watch it!" his grandmother hollered while playfully slapping him behind the head. Mayruhk whined for a bit, shielding his head with both hands and tilting away from her. "Ooh, please boy," she said with a limp hand and sauntered off.

Mayruhk took a moment to recover as he laid against the table and watched the still screen. A micro flash caused him to sit up while he monitored the new email that was delivered to his inbox. "I'ma take a break," he announced without a change in position.

Soon, he slowly reached forward and gently went through the motions to clear the open pages. "Yeah, forget this. Don't make no sense... don't make no sense." The brightly lit colors faded away and became absent in his presence. He followed his actions with a short sigh, while his eyes darted to the left with no target in mind.

* * *

The sound of bone lightly tapping a hard surface soon became prominent as Josiah waved his right hand around his hip area. "Shit," he mumbled to himself and stretched down to a handle sewn onto the top of the bag.

Josiah lifted and slipped his arm through the handles, and then reached for the last one as he held the door open. The door was light, and didn't have much resistance as he fell forward and stumbled into the house. He took his time quietly removing his sneakers with a couple movements, slipping them from the toes and heel of each foot. After the challenge was complete, he examined the open living area and attempted to search the visible portion of the kitchen. "Hello?" he shouted without enthusiasm, and shut the door behind him.

"Hello Josiah!" an older woman's voice replied from a short distance away over the sound of shuffled papers.

Josiah continued as if nothing alarmed him and set the bags in the kitchen. He opened the refrigerator with a sigh and stood there for a moment to study what was already occupying space.

"Did you get my care bars?" the woman asked.

Josiah stopped suddenly after the completion of the question, as if the sound had attracted unwanted attention. "I got the apple cinnamon and caramel... umm, caramel-tastic, or something like that. They didn't have the cocoa one."

"That's fine," she answered in approval of his decision. "What about my juice?"

"I didn't get it," Josiah answered without sympathy.

"They ran out?" shouted the woman, appalled by the information.

Josiah snickered to himself. "No, I just didn't buy it."

"Why?" she asked.

"Not enough..." he replied and shook his head before he continued to put the groceries away. "Just leave me alone..." he whispered under his breath.

It didn't take long for him to finish his task, and he immediately crept past two doors to dash up a set of stairs on the balls of his feet. But before he reached the top step, he planted his left foot and slightly turned his upper body. "Oh yeah, Mom!" Josiah called and then waited until his mother used a vocal sound to signal her attentiveness. "Dad said he will be in late today!"

"He said he's working his second job?" the woman asked.

Josiah shook his head. "No, at least not that I remember!"

"Okay, you picking him up, or you want me to get him?"

"No, you're good, I'm usually up at two anyway, so I should be good!" Josiah replied, and continued his original journey. "I have the keys!"

"Okay!" she replied. "Wait... did you hear back from the jobs?"

Josiah over-expressed the cringe that the sound of the question brought him. He hesitated, but after a deep breath, he finally responded. "I haven't heard anything yet. But I've been sending applications to hospitals and labs, and even applied for an internship... all they said was they'll let me know. But I'ma call again on Monday to check on the process and see if there are more offers," Josiah explained, hanging his head and constantly rubbing his temple with his left hand.

"Okay!"

Josiah stumbled across the small hall to a door that he easily pushed open. He walked in and threw himself on his bed. "Fuck," he said to himself as he pushed himself up and stumbled out the room. "I need to get the hell up outta here... shit's not good for my health," he mumbled under his breath as he pressed open another door a couple steps from his room.

The interior was detailed, with tiles arranged neatly halfway up the surrounding wall until the design transitioned to a cream-colored coat of paint. The only disturbance to the symmetry existed in the form of a white toilet, a sink with reflective knobs, and bathtub with a silver overhead.

Josiah instinctively aimed for the sink and turned the knobs; he stared into the mirror for a second, and then shied away from the reflection. His sole focus soon became the cloudy water as it conformed to the details of his hands and fingers. He rubbed the extra water on his face and shut his eyes to reach for a rag hanging in the far-right corner of the room, past the curtain of the shower.

He rubbed his face with the rag, making sure to clean the individual sections, but not once using his reflection for guidance. "Ugh," he sighed, and ran the rag through the water. He kept his eyes closed until the cloth passed over to wipe the collection of small bubbles and white foam. "Gotta go, gotta go. I need to get my black ass outta here," he said until his eyes met with his reflection.

Josiah stood hypnotized for a moment, and his pupils began to focus on the details of his face. He picked at the small scar beneath his right pupil and the varying sizes of bumps on his easily irritated skin. Held by emotion, he delayed his current actions and placed both hands firmly on the sink base. "I *must* have a place of my own and have freedom," he stated, and focused on his image in the mirror. He squinted his eyes and proclaimed, "I have a job that gives me the flexibility to study and obtain my doctorate. I have my own two-bedroom condominium in Queens that is almost paid off and my blue coupe is in the driveway." Josiah closed his eyes and held his position.

Shortly after, he reached in his pocket and scrolled through his phone while exiting the bathroom. He took his time, despite how few steps he needed to enter his bedroom. He paused at the entryway and used his other hand to pinch and double tap the screen until he found satisfaction and paid attention to his path at his convenience.

Finally, the backs of his knees bent slightly as they collided with the soft edge of the mattress. The collision didn't alarm him, but after a few taps on his phone, he studied his environment before removing his pants quickly and hovered them over the floor. He aimed to his right in order to find a target, and began to swing his arm left to right until he released it from his grasp.

\* \* \*

A thud sounded as Mayruhk's bag landed on the seat closest to one corner of the waiting area. He searched the small hallway and chose to sit in the cushioned chair glued to the corner by the office door. Instinctively, he stuck his hand in his pocket and drew out his phone before he adjusted his dark blue tie and situated himself. He leaned gently on his left elbow, but soon released the tension on his sensitive nerves and checked the sleeve of his color-coordinated suit.

"Hey, how you doing, man?" asked an unexpected voice. "Are you here for an interview with Mr. Amir?"

Mayruhk's eyes darted to his right and studied the meek figure of a man as he waited for an answer. He didn't bother to turn his head. "Yes," he responded, and immediately resumed interaction with his phone's display.

"Thank you," the man said with no return for his politeness. "I'm sorry, my name is Jamal." He stepped forward with more confidence and an extended right hand.

In response, Mayruhk became fully attentive to the man as his frame continued to engulf the background. Mayruhk dropped his phone in the unoccupied seat beside him with his body fully facing Jamal. When Jamal approached him, Mayruhk stood up without a comment. "Mayruhk," he finally admitted with a strong grip as he glared at the man in the eyes.

"May, Rule?" Jamal asked with an ignorant tone and cocked his head slightly.

"Ma. Ruk," Mayruhk repeated with emphasis while guiding his body back to the chair. He picked up his phone and proceeded to gently tap at the screen with his thumb, but occasionally glanced up at the towering man, whose positive attitude seemed permanent to his character.

Jamal stood for a moment, and then sat a couple seats down in the row parallel Mayruhk's. Silence soon set over the small area, but neither inhabitant chose to break from self-isolation. A few minutes went by before Jamal placed his phone on his thigh and began to tap a beat on the back of the phone. It only took a few seconds before the sounds caught Mayruhk's attention, as he now viciously stared at Jamal.

"Sorry," Jamal apologized as he witnessed Mayruhk roll his eyes. He remained silent for a moment as he struggled to keep his head still.

"Excuse me... excuse me." Mayruhk darted his eyes up again in response to the call. "Sorry, excuse me." Jamal said with sincerity. "Do you know why you're here, or you just want a paycheck?

Mayruhk hesitated to answer. "I want a paycheck."

"Oh... wow," Jamal responded. "No, I'm only asking because... well, for me, I heard that this was, you know, to be social and help people. Like, what brought you here?"

Mayruhk stared at the man with squinted eyes until his held expression relaxed. "An Uber," he answered with a monotone voice that only a robot could challenge for the least amount of emotion.

Jamal laughed subtly. "Okay... I mean, from what I know, you must interact with multiple people, so I was just wondering if you done something like a liaison position before, or maybe you love the black community... ?"

"No, I wanted a job," Mayruhk said, paired with a dry and uninterested attitude.

"Mmm," Jamal replied. "I wanted to help out our community, but I don't know, because we participate in some crazy stuff. So, I feel like I have to take care of me, and you know, if I have enough left over... I do want to give back to a charity or something. I can see that."

Mayruhk remained quiet. "That's nice," he finally replied, not paying Jamal any more attention than it cost while he waited his appointment.

\* \* \*

Josiah sucked his teeth in disgust. "It's better than my reason," he said in response to a chuckling Jamal.

"You never know," Jamal rebutted, leaning back into the chair across from Josiah. "It's funny, because I was talking with a dude about a week ago, you know, just regular talk. Let's just say he probably couldn't care less."

"I feel you; it be like that," Josiah replied while rubbing his chin. "But nah. I was going to say yeah, I just needed something until I can finish my master's."

"What are you getting your master's in?" Jamal asked.

"Chemical engineering," Josiah said with bolstering confidence.

"Oh... okay," Jamal said with a couple of blinks adding to his bemused expression. "What made you take this job again? You sound like you should be saving the world. Jeez, chemical engineering."

Josiah laughed and lent forward rubbing his palms. "I don't know about saving the world, but I do want to collaborate with other scientists and engineers to make technology that will help advance the physical abilities of people in the black community. I have other plans to advance technology by understanding the best reactions for efficient environmental control and ways to counter cancers and diseases."

"That's dope." Jamal responded while nodding his head. "What made you get into... um... chemical engineering?"

Josiah let out a breathy laugh through his nostrils. "I got you." He smiled after his comment as he studied some of the pleasant features of the room. "Well, my pops is a detective, and he would tell me stories about—well, long story short—a lot of the things that messed-up individuals and cops want to claim to be threatened by us, but if we build something and do well without them, it's a... an issue. Excuse me. So, I wanted to make things that only Africans can use, and make digestible chemicals that can speed the recovery process from fatal wounds or deflect bullets—things that are only adaptable to African descendants."

"Oh nice, so you're trying to turn the world into superheroes. I'm sorry, why only black people?" Jamal asked.

Josiah laughed without restriction. "Nah, I just want to balance things out so it's harder to kill or steal from us. I just want to give America a reason to think twice when they send their guard dogs or allow other people to destroy what we built again and then play victim," he added, but his attention was taken by the sound of a rotating doorknob.

Duke stepped into the doorway, filling the void with his large muscular build. He grinned while squinting both eyes as if excitement was the only emotion he knew. "Mr. Williams?" he asked, a careful onlooker to the short hallway occupied by both gentlemen.

"Yes," Josiah answered and eagerly stood up.

Duke continued his heartwarming engagement as he shook Josiah's hand, and then allowed him to enter before following. "How are you doing so far? I understand it may be early for most," Duke said as he located a couple items in the drawers of his desk and placed them on top in preparation to sit in his leather armchair.

Josiah quickly became immersed in the decorative value of the small office. His movements slowed as he reached for the dark wooden armrest.

"You okay?" Duke asked, resting comfortably as if he were on a plush brown yacht with a vanilla sea behind him.

"Yes," Josiah answered, and straightened up for a moment as he became aware of Duke's raised brow. As he sat down, he shifted his attention to the organized desk, visibly covered with a desktop, paper scanner, and the recently added papers.

"To start, I would like to formally introduce myself as Mr. Amir. Please refer to me as such, unless stated otherwise. I would also add that per agreement in your application, I have studied your resume and all media you have allowed me to access with the purpose of gaining an idea of who I am dealing with. Understood?" Duke finished while observing Josiah's energetic demeanor.

"Yes," Josiah responded while his oxford shoe tapped on the hardwood floor.

"Okay," Duke said with a large grin. "I learned that you have collegiate experience in chemical engineering and philanthropy. With those unintentionally being the highlights of your career, how will your skills advance this company and its goals?" Duke asked, shifting his attention from Josiah to the paper that laid on his desk.

Josiah glanced to his right. "Excuse me for a second," he said respectfully.

"No, take your time. This is one of many important decisions in life, and should be treated as such," Duke responded and leaned slightly in his chair. His elbow made a small thump as it landed on the table to support his chin.

"Thank you," Josiah said. "I believe this company has had arguably an impactful role in supporting and investing in the black businesses of America. I'm not business savvy, but I do understand philanthropy to a degree, and how to communicate with scientists that are supported by your company. I aspire to grow with the preexisting companies in order to strengthen the impact on the community... positively. Excuse me. I also want to introduce ideas and projects created from my experience and originality, and collaborate with other like-minded or better-suited individuals to create new businesses and charities that work to remedy most problems African descendants face."

Duke nodded. "I understand," he said as verbal confirmation that he was listening. "What are some ideas you are looking to invest in as a chemical engineer?" Duke then asked, exchanging his attention between the paper and Josiah again.

"I've studied the chemical reactions that exist in the human body. Mainly the African body. My goal is to create a chemical reaction that will enhance the resilience of the body to pain and fatal trauma in order to decrease the death toll and unlawful assaults. I believe this would deter officers from attacking or being able to kill someone, knowing that something was invented to make African descendants more resilient to daily troubles." Josiah paused for a second. "I understand it may take a long time to achieve that, but that is something I want to work towards."

"Oh wow, what inspired you to want to create that?" Duke asked. He squinted his eyes and leaned forward while rubbing his chin.

"My father is a detective in the city. I grew up hearing a lot of stories about abuse from the law officers in black communities, and even how they treated their own officers before. But, um, something happened..." Josiah began, but stopped his speech immediately. He averted his eyes downward and rubbed his hands together between his shaking legs. His blinking became more frequent. "Excuse me," Josiah finally said after a brief period of silence. "But, um... um, I don't want anything to happen to him again. Also... I have a degree in chemical engineering, and I'm good with... mixing chemicals." Josiah said, but stared at the hardwood floor as if caught in a daze.

"I saw you used to teach karate in middle school," Duke said immediately. "How was that experience?"

"Huh?" Josiah answered with a whisper.

"The karate program... at your old middle school. You sent an article about it." Duke explained as he studied Josiah squinted and finally changed his focus.

Josiah's eyes wandered up slowly as he broke out of his trance. Confused, he focused on Duke's widened eyes, which portrayed a man vulnerable to the change of emotional atmosphere. Josiah squinted his eyes. "Wait, I'm sorry, I'm lost."

"No, you're not," Duke responded. "I made a mistake, but I genuinely do want to know what that experience was like."

"Mmm," Josiah responded, nodding his head. "I loved it. I guess... I guess it's because I felt special. I could do things that weren't, um, average."

"I'd say so." Duke interrupted. "I could only imagine this little version of you teaching people bigger than him to beat people bigger than them," Duke finished with a chuckle, but muffled most of the sound with his hand.

Josiah couldn't help but smile. He shifted his focus away from Duke to gather himself. "Yeah, I guess in theory I was usually right. And my sensei had my back."

"Are you and your sensei still close?" Duke asked.

"Yeah," Josiah said with reserved excitement. "I still train under him and teach classes," Josiah continued, and immediately lost himself in the lower half of Duke's desk until his eyes widened and locked onto Duke.

Duke smirked. "Don't worry about it. I'm just glad you feel comfortable now, but may I proceed?" Duke asked, his closed smile soon turned upside down.

Josiah straightened up in the seat, which caused it to jerk forward on the floor. He exhaled deeply. "Yes."

"Good," Duke responded as his eyes returned to the paper set in front of him. "I want to play out a scenario..." Duke added, but was focused on mouthing the text quickly to himself. "What do you believe you will offer to this company with the position?"

Josiah took a staggered breath and then angled his pressed lips toward the top corner of his mouth. "I offer... um, experienced communication due to my past as a student philanthropist. I worked well with people despite their personalities, and I'm aware of when and where I would take over as the leader or follower. I created new programs and assisted with some, because I was told that I have a vibe that inspires people to want to act and believe in me. I will offer new ideas with the people I interact with and understand what can be done so that the people involved will grow."

"Thank you for that; it sounds honest," Duke replied with a slight nod and a blink of his eyes. "Would you like to ask me any questions?" his question followed with a more oral resonance in his voice.

Josiah paused for a moment, but a gasp slipped through until he forced himself to breathe instead. "Not at the moment, but may I contact you if I do?"

"Of course!" Duke said, and abruptly lifted a small card off the table. As Josiah reached forward, he continued. "I know you're young, but you know."

"Thank you," Josiah said in a hushed tone. He sat down with controlled grace as the card slid into his pocket, unseen due to the wall of copper colored flesh.

Duke rose in synchronization with his prospective liaison. "Well," he said as he buttoned his jacket, and then swept his hand across the lower half, followed by a gesture toward the door.

Josiah picked himself up with haste and shuffled around his chair to reverse his former course. He could hear the tapping from Duke's shoes and a rustling of papers paired with the noise of moving drawers. Curiosity consumed him, but he met a few inches from a man's towering figure. "Oh!" he exclaimed and exited with an open door. "Have a good one," he said as he passed Jamal, who nodded and held focus until Josiah turned the corner.

* * *

"Mr. Manning?" Duke asked, standing confidently in his gray suit coupled with a similar-colored tie and white shirt.

"Yes," replied Mayruhk as he quickly hid his phone, allowing his free hands to press himself forward. "Excuse me, but do you mind if I bring my bag in with me?" he asked innocently as he grasped firmly on the top of the small book bag.

"Of course not," Duke responded with squinted eyes. "When you're ready, please follow me."

Mayruhk took a moment to study the area while he stood with his bag tightly held. After one glance over to Jamal, he proceeded to push past the slightly open door without a word. He entered with caution, observing every inch. He soaked in the vanilla-coated walls as he slowly became immersed in the bright, euphoric atmosphere. Two armchairs stationed in front of an average-sized desk enticed him to sit, but a small gesture from the owner made the process quicker.

"Good morning!" Duke said with excitement, like a child at his favorite celebration.

"Good morning," Mayruhk responded, but his own greeting carried a slight resemblance to an annoyed teenage brother. He set his bag down beside him, but made no effort to remove attention from Duke's process of studying certain documents on his dark wooden table.

"Ah," Duke said, alarming Mayruhk to what he may say next. "Virginia, right? Nor-folk."

"Mm, yessir." Mayruhk answered. "Nor-fuhk," he admitted, confidently pronouncing his city with a thick accent.

Duke smiled. "How was the trip?"

Mayruhk immediately began to nod his head in response. "It was real good, thank you again," he explained with the utmost gratitude.

"That's good, that's good, and no problem," Duke said with a bright smile. "Dre treated you okay?"

"Yes," Mayruhk answered. "He said he'll wait outside so I wouldn't have to wait after," Mayruhk continued, now focused on African inspired objects that decorated the room.

"Okay wow, that was nice of him," Duke said as he continued with his positive demeanor. "But... I would like to get started," he said, and Mayruhk responded with a few slight nods of his head.

"What do you aspire to do as part of the company?" Duke asked.

With little hesitation, Mayruhk responded, "I aspire to use my position as a liaison to influence the narrative that has been given to the black community. I want to use my extensive knowledge in business to collaborate with current businesses, and build relationships with new ones to help lower the statistics that correlate employment of a person of African descent and the possibility of holding onto or growing in social and financial status in relation to the workplace. I want to prove that the stereotypes created are false; that the blacks that weren't hired due to name or hair can and will showcase vastly superior diligence compared to those they chose out of ignorance and racism."

"Well spoken," Duke admitted. "In being here, I assume that our thoughts are aligned based on the information you sent me, but I'm glad to know that in person you match what you want to portray. I tend to gaze upon the big picture of it all. What you said does coordinate well with my ideals, but are you more focused on the big picture, or are you detailed-oriented?"

"I would say... I am detail-oriented," Mayruhk answered confidently. "I don't overlook the big picture of my journey, but I am the type to make sure everything is well-placed and organized before I move on to the next thing that will get me to the main goal."

"Mm, okay," Duke said. "I referenced that because I feel that it's good to have both. So, I'm going to use that to go into my next question; how do you deal with stressful situations when pursuing a goal?"

"Typically, I like to slow things down in my head. I take in as much information as I can, and stay calm through the process. Then I look at as many perspectives as possible and keep an open mind to other critiques." Mayruhk paused with his mouth minutely ajar.

"Okay," Duke said after a brief pause in the discussion. "Does that normally take a while to solve the problem?"

"It depends on the severity of it, but I try not to be upset if it isn't perfect," Mayruhk explained without a second of time between the statements.

Duke nodded with a raised brow until his eyes finally met Mayruhk's. "I can agree with that," he responded, and then gathered his papers together. "Well, do you have any questions for me or any requests while you're in the city?" he asked with a smile.

"No, but thank you for everything you have done, and for awarding me this opportunity," Mayruhk answered, and immediately grabbed his bag to place it in his lap.

Duke chuckled as Mayruhk rose to his feet. "No, I understand. You came to conquer and then go home," Duke teased.

Mayruhk respectfully smirked with an added bow of the head. "I guess you say that."

Duke nodded in response. "Well, you seem like a highly intelligent young man, and I wish you the best in the future. May it be here or wherever," Duke finished with a chuckle, and momentarily watched as Mayruhk began his exit.

As Mayruhk approached the door, he couldn't fight the urge to admire the resemblance it had to his grandmother's. The African American flag hung confidently where it was fastened, and it instantly made him think of home.

\* \* \*

Mayruhk swung the door open and pulled his bag up to his chest. He reached in and pulled out his laptop with care, then balanced it on top of the improvised table.

"Grandma!" Mayruhk shouted excitedly as he rushed into his grandmother's room. She moved with limited effort as Mayruhk crashed onto her knitted blanket. "I got the job."

"You don't get to burst in like that during my afternoon programs," she said, and turned to follow the actions of realistic characters as they played a role.

"Dang Grandma," Mayruhk gasped. "I out of V.A. for one day and you lost all your love for me!"

"Could've said something instead of falling asleep when you were probably sleeping there and back," his grandmother argued.

"You were out cold and I got in like one in the morning Grandma!" Mayruhk countered with his own remark and a bright smile. "Uh uh, don't do me like that."

With a slight pause, she finally turned off the cable box. "What is it, boy?"

Mayruhk laughed. "Okay, look, Grandma," he managed to say, and turned the monitor away from himself. He peered over the side like a noisy cat and tapped at the touch screen. "See, I got the job," he explained after he highlighted certain text in yellow.

"Oooh." His grandmother placed the computer on her lap, read silently, and nodded her head at times. "So, let me get this straight. They're gonna have you running around all over the country to act as a representative of this man?"

"Yes, but I mean, he just wants us to organize and facilitate programs and partnerships. It's a way to stay involved with philanthropy and develop the financial and social activities in the black community with his advice," he explained as he received the laptop. "Plus, he's covering most of our bills and necessities as a part of it."

"Us?" she asked.

"Mm-hmm," Mayruhk responded with his head almost submerged in the mouth of his computer. "The job said two positions, but I'll meet the other person next week."

"Mm, and don't think money is going to persuade me into sending you all over the country." She sighed and moved subtly with unease. "But, Chattanooga, huh."

"You okay?" Mayruhk asked, averting his eyes from his screen for a split-second.

"No," she answered without hesitation. "I've heard some things about Tennessee... I just don't remember where not to go."

"Oooh..."

"Make sure you let me know where you're going, keep your location on, and stay with your co-worker," his grandmother demanded as her tone shifted the atmosphere.

Mayruhk gave her his full attention. "I will, Grandma," he agreed with added sentiment.

"So, how do you feel about going?" she asked.

* * *

"I'm thinking about it, he wants us to travel a lot," Josiah answered his father's question. He corrected his body posture to lean back on the concrete steps for support. His eyes wandered across the shades of green and light brown until he lost concentration. "I just don't know about representing a company, especially with the history of this one."

His father sat beside him with a puzzled look. He graced the railing with his hand and cleared his throat. "Well, growing up, Duke Amir was active in many of the communities, and used many of those qualities in his company. I'm pretty sure he has an understanding and a certain knowledge about how he wants to accomplish his goals. Which I believe is something similar to what you said you wanted to do." his father paused for a second and then examined the attentive young man. "So, I think that if he chose you to lead, or even be in a position to have any type of control over his goal, he knows the decision he made. Plus, you even said you'll have an opportunity to work on your dreams, too."

Josiah smirked in response. "Yeah," he said, and then cleared his throat. "You're right."

"I think it's a great company to work for, and I've heard a lot that they've done for our community in the past." His father let his head hang for a moment. "I understand you've been carrying yourself like you have nothing to offer."

Skepticism took to Josiah's face like a paper mask fixed to a stick.

"Don't argue with me. But I think this will be a great opportunity for you to gather yourself and gain a little control so you can have the freedom to do what you want." Josiah's father paused for a second. "I believe you will accomplish great things. I like to think that your life is a manifestation of what I wanted, and what I saw would bring a positive energy to this world."

Josiah stared at the ground, refusing to face the emotional burden being placed upon him. After a short while, Josiah peered into the eyes of his father, who wouldn't fold and who kept a joyous expression. His father chuckled and stood up with an open palm for direction. "Go show them what you can do," he said.

Josiah pushed himself up and stood by his father's side with confidence. Without warning, his father embraced him in his arms and then pushed him behind his head. Josiah stumbled up the stairs, laughing until he gained his footing. He closed his eyes while he caught his breath after the series of accidents that almost happened. When he reached the top, he found a brief opportunity to close his eyes and envision where he would be in just a few short weeks.

\* \* \*

Josiah opened his eyes with a squint to witness the amount of ascension needed to reach the open door to the black jet. He balanced himself on the metal rods as he wiped the dust blown into his eyes before he continued up the stairs, his hand pressed firmly against his dark gray suit with dark blue highlights from his tie and pocket square. Finally, he rushed through the entryway, but the brief shock of embarrassment hit his stomach when his eye caught a glimpse of a young man seated and well-prepared in a classic black and white ensemble.

"What's good?" Josiah said as he stepped onto the plane. He was soon mesmerized by the polished look of the jet's interior. Another step, and he felt mentally trapped within the strip of burgundy that ran between cognac furniture until it stopped by the black door.

"What's up, bro?" Mayruhk responded as he lowered his phone. He rested comfortably on his pristine leather throne coupled with a table off to his right.

Without another word, Josiah reached out his hand with a slight lean until Mayruhk slapped his hand on top and slid his fingers into a tight link. "Josiah, my fault," he said over the sound of Mayruhk's snap. He then hovered over the other chair and let his body fall into it.

Mayruhk waved his hand in response. "Bro, I'm not worried about that, bro," he responded, and proceeded to rub his arm while he paid attention to Josiah, now sitting blissfully in the chair.

"Where you from?" Josiah asked, and then looked over with barely open eyelids.

"Norfolk." Mayruhk said proudly as Josiah sat up a little.

"Oh, word; where's that at?" Josiah asked while he searched his chair briefly and then fastened his seatbelt.

Mayruhk targeted his co-worker with devilish eyes. "It's in Virginia," he answered with little regard for the other's childlike innocence.

Josiah paused for a moment. "Oh shoot," he said through a chuckle. "Nah, I got you; my fault, but nah, my mom used to work down there when she was younger," he said as his eyes wandered to the ground.

"Oh," Mayruhk responded immediately. He watched Josiah fulfill his curiosity as he studied the room from his perspective. "What did she do, if you don't mind me asking?"

Josiah focused for a moment and stared at the tan roof of the plane. "Mmm... Navy."

"Ooo okay, that's cool," Mayruhk said, easing back into his seat. "Your family from V.A.?" Mayruhk asked.

"Oh, nah!" Josiah answered. "Nah, we from here, it's just after college; I think she stayed down there for a bit and then came back up when she met my pops."

"Oh, true, true," Mayruhk responded, and then peered out the window.

"You, uh... you ever done something like this before?" Josiah asked, easing into the question slowly.

"No," Mayruhk answered while shaking his head. He then studied the passing terrain of a lime and brown mix until the scenery transitioned into a larger portrait of intricate patterns. "You?" he finally asked before properly facing his co-worker.

"Nah!" Josiah said instantly. "I mean, but aside from having a degree, it seems pretty simple, right?"

"Yeah," Mayruhk agreed, and then placed his phone on the table nearest him.

"Yeah, word." Josiah said. "They just want us to go sell some stuff and speak on the business, right?" he added, and then watched as Mayruhk nodded his head in response.

"Did you read the report about Ms. Jacobs and what we gotta do?" Mayruhk asked.

"Yeah, but yooo, did you see her, my guy?" Josiah said, with a raising pitch that illustrated his excitement.

"I 'unno, bro," Mayruhk argued as he rolled his eyes and then couldn't control his smile. "Usually the crazy ones are pretty as hell."

"Facts!" Josiah exclaimed. "But real talk though, I wonder what she's like in person."

* * *

"Good afternoon," a woman said confidently in her native accent. The two men soon found their attention taken by an approaching copper-toned woman, about average height, whose reflective dark skin tone was complemented by a light yellow body con dress. She then held her hand out, but the forward shift in momentum caused a few strands of her hair to cover her right eye. She laughed as she quickly waved the strands away. "I'm Etana Jacobs," she said gleefully as she continued with her formal introduction.

"Good Afternoon," Josiah replied immediately, paying close attention to the host.

"Hey, how are you doing." Mayruhk said shortly after, taking a second to give admiration before he continued to let his eyes wander between the land occupied with tents and the two approaching men behind Etana. "I'm sorry. Mr. Amir wanted us to deliver this with apologies for his absence," Mayruhk added, and then held out a small box supported.

Etana smirked. "Aww, he didn't have to." She took the gift and held it in the air off to her side until the nearest man removed it. "I have to remember to send a 'thank you' card before things get too hectic. Thank you." She finished with a showing of her bright top row of teeth.

Mayruhk replied with a slight nod.

Etana swayed forward with a slight raise in one of her eyebrows. "So, from what was discussed, you two are new to something like this?" she asked, and then glanced upward for a short time. "Actually, this whole position is new, am I correct?"

"Yeah," Josiah instantly responded while nodding his head. He turned to Mayruhk, who remained quiet, and then faced forward, putting his hands deep in his pockets.

"I understand, but because I never spoke with the both of you about what I'm about and what I want to accomplish today, I would like to speak a little about that, especially that you're here early and making a great impression on behalf of your company. I want to relay an understanding so that we as a team are unified in what goal we are working towards," Etana explained as her focus changed from Josiah to Mayruhk at a constant pace. "Also, I would like to note that Duke, his family, and I have a different relationship than what I have with you, so I would like to know what you believe is going to happen based on your briefing."

Josiah opened his mouth, but settled with making a breathy sigh. He then looked to Mayruhk, who glanced back in response. "From what I understand..." Mayruhk began, and then cleared his throat behind a clenched fist. "You have invested heavily into the development and empowerment of the black population in this town, from what started in realty to financial investment and marketing support for local, black-owned businesses and stores." Mayruhk focused on Etana's uninterested expression. "But what you want to do today is enlist the help of local businesses to invest in adding African history to the town's local historical curriculum and host programs that teach it for free."

"Yes," Etana replied, now nonverbally invested in the discussion. "Y'all have most of it. I assume the both of you share that?" she asked as her eyes pointed in the direction of Josiah.

"Our job is to strengthen the partnership with current as well as incoming companies. Do you also want us to market the mission to consumers, or continue our focus on helping to create, market, and finance companies?" Josiah competed and maintained a stoic expression. "As well as encourage the self-defense programs and investment into them?"

Etana smiled, and then nodded like a bouncing ball on subtitles.

"Putting this together, I kept in mind your visibility in relation to the audience and their predicted movement patterns. You aren't positioned directly by the entrance, but you are accommodated with two motion posters, recognition on the forefront of tickets and the tablets, and seated at the head of other attractions where the most traffic is predicted," she stated, continuing her entrance into the bordered-off area. "Questions so far?" she asked, spinning around and then passing the gift to a passing worker. "Thank you!"

She then turned back to the men, continuing, "Your kiosk is the third one down. All of your materials will be under the table, resealed." Etana scanned over the face of her tablet, quietly tapping mostly where cheeks could be. "Any questions?" she asked, seconds before looking towards the entrance and then focusing on her audience.

"No," Josiah replied while Mayruhk shook his head.

"Good." She wiped her tablet with a cloth that seemed to appear from underneath. With an added nod, Etana directed her guest toward the entry to the enclosed field. She continued a short distance past the custom check-in station, where a member of security stood patiently. "Well, this is you. Please excuse me, but don't hesitate to ask questions." Etana said as she demonstrated a dramatic reveal, her free hand waving gracefully across the air to showcase the term *Amirnation* emboldened on the fabric of the central tent.

"Thank you," they said as approached the group of organized boxes set on the table.

Etana nodded, and then redirected to four men that were waiting by the gate, which cued Josiah and Mayruhk to inspect the multiple items at their kiosk. Boxes were rummaged through as if curious children were assigned to the task until the table was bare, tinted a seemingly darker shade of gray due to the overcast from the tarp above.

Mayruhk discovered there were a stack of balloons, and waved them a short distance from Josiah's face. "Does she expect us to blow these up with lung power?" Josiah responded, looking around after his sarcastic remark.

"I guess so, bro." Mayruhk replied as he continued to fully empty the cardboard boxes and toss them to the ground. "For real, for real, I don't think they care if we use 'em or not."

"I don't see a pump. But I mean, she has some blown up over there." Josiah surveyed the outside of the tented area before he placed his hands in his pockets. "I'll go ask real quick. I guess you can see what else there is, and if we need anything else, ya feel me?"

"Ight," Mayruhk replied as Josiah began to walk over to Etana, who was still caught in conversation.

Josiah paid close attention to the details of the field. There were subtle differences between each tent, from the font and color of the company name to the number of boxes placed in any possible area nearest the set table. His eyes wandered until they fell upon the backs of Etana and her security.

The number of backs quickly changed, and Etana was back by one of her approaching guards as he took over interaction with the new guest. The atmosphere quickly shifted as their voices raised, and the men in front of Etana immediately brought their hands to their side until a series of loud pops dispersed the crowd. Etana's team went limp, along with a member of the opposite force.

Etana cursed in panic. "The F!!" Mayruhk shouted as he turned to witness Etana use her tablet to deter her assailants. After a brief analysis, he ducked under the table and flipped it on the side.

Josiah stumbled back as Etana was dragged away by her wrist, like captured prey attempting to use its last reserve of strength to free itself. He slowly began to take complete steps without distributing any of his attention to his surroundings, until a glare captured his eye. Josiah ducked and ran to his left quickly, his arm folded to protect the side of his head.

A loud clash of metal echoed through the open field. "Mm," Josiah anticipated with a tightened his fist and running form. But after the sudden realization that there wasn't any impact to his body, he made himself vulnerable in exchange for the sight of a confused lone wolf while the rest of the pack loaded the unmarked van's cargo space.

A small hand gesture from the predator signaled Josiah to act, and he pursued the possible safety from the array of tables and tents rather than the fenced perimeter a shorter distance away. Instantly, the man rocketed towards Josiah's destination with a lowered body, a metal extension protruding from his palm on the side opposite the thumb.

As the distance closed, the man retreated at an angle and threw another attempted shot with a blinding jab. Josiah tucked his chin and added extra protection with a raised shoulder and folded arms glued to his ear. He focused heavily on the weapon while shifting around obstacles and occasionally using them to keep any injuries he received minor.

Josiah soon found an opportunity to lower his center, and aggressively rammed his shoulder into the man's solar plexus. Like a gator, he latched to the attacker's arm and ripped the knife free, but tossed it carelessly.

"Shit!" he exclaimed, and then faked low after he noticed a change in the man's direction toward him, then attacked with a left-handed reverse punch followed by an elbow to the head. Instantly, the man countered by wrapping his arms around Josiah's upper body.

Josiah struggled until he landed a knee to a vital area and pushed the man off his body. The set up was followed by a hammer fist to the outer thigh of the stunned opponent that made him bend while Josiah stepped to an angle and hook kicked the back of the man's head.

Josiah stopped for a moment and scanned the area until he caught a glimpse of the top of his co-worker's head.

Mayruhk revealed himself from behind the unorthodox table, but only to show his full facial identity. He gaped as an exhausted Josiah walked toward him until he panned over the field and spotted one of the men return from the van and pull out a gun.

"Ay, get down and run!" Mayruhk shouted to gain a reaction from Josiah, who ran in a random pattern with a lowered base and covered head. The man let off a couple shots until he stopped with visible frustration, and then changed targets after a quick reload. Mayruhk dropped behind the table and rolled to the side, his teeth clenched and his hands squeezed the top of his head as his body filled with anxiety.

Soon, only the roar of the van's engine sounded through the tension-filled air. Mayruhk lifted his head before shifting to his left and peered through the widest hole to become a witness to his attacker's wounded retreat. After a short distance, the back tires burst simultaneously and forced the vehicle to slowly dig into the soil as it came to a halt.

Mayruhk continued to watch as he changed his focus between the van and the open area where Josiah once stood, until he noticed a difference. A bright red dot centered itself at the center of the right van door. Mayruhk scoped around to spot who was using the laser, but became momentarily blinded by a flashing light when his eyes traveled too far to the right. Without warning, the buzz of his phone took his attention and raised his heart rate as he fished for it with shaky hands.

*We are with Ms. Etana Jacobs' back-up security team. Go save Ms. Jacobs,* was written in his notification center. *Please,* soon followed.

Mayruhk frantically pressed on the lower half of his phone and started an automated response that speed-dialed 911. He peered over the table and fell for the same trick that blinded him the first time

"Hello?" answered the dispatch woman.

"Someone's being kidnapped, and they shot people!" he shouted into the mic.

"Okay, do you give me permission to track your location?" she asked with the sounds of keyboard clicks in the background.

"Uh... sure?" Mayruhk responded, confused

"Yes?" the woman corrected.

"Yes," Mayruhk answered, and pulled his phone from his ear as it continued to vibrate.

*Your partner is fine btw, but we need you to do us a favor and free Ms. Jacobs. You will be protected from weapons and be safe, or they will believe you slowed their plans.*

Mayruhk quickly looked over the table. One man inched toward Mayruhk's general location while his partner studied the van's rear.

Mayruhk pressed his right heel into the dirt, but fell forward onto his palms as he studied the open area beyond the small gate.

His mouth dropped open as thoughts of death raced through his mind. "Fuck." He cried softly and dug his fingers into the dirt.

Mayruhk closed his eyes and took deep breaths despite his steadily increasing heartrate. Without hesitation, he pressed against the table and launched it as the target approached. He dashed to the right before he rushed his opponent and dug through the man's thick jacket to grip his muscle, and then performed a shoulder throw and slammed the man to the ground.

Mayruhk checked around and wrestled with the man to gain top position. The man threw an array of punches aimed at Mayruhk's arms and obliques while he coughed heavily. Mayruhk fought through the punches to grab his opponent's arm, but the man forced his forearm into Mayruhk's cheek. He searched the man's upper body again and then performed *omoplata* on the vulnerable arm and dislocated the man's shoulder.

A quick transition to a turtle choke siphoned the cries of pain from Mayruhk's opponent, but a loud thud replaced the dominant sound in the area. Mayruhk turned his cheek to see the driver appear from beside the van. Anger enveloped his physical expression and he charged forward, but Josiah leapt into view and led with a furious drop kick to the man's trapezius.

Josiah followed with a multitude of elbows to the head until the man was unconscious. "Ugh!" he cried with his nose aimed to the sky before he crawled away from his victim.

Mayruhk walked up to check on him, but lacked in proper posture. He looked to the door handle to the van and then tended to his partner.

"I'm straight," mumbled Josiah as he massaged his forehead.

Hesitantly, Mayruhk opened the door, making sure to keep the door close to his chest and step to the side. The sound of a distressed Etana banging on anything around her caught his attention, forcing him to slowly peer in after a quick look to satisfy the need for precaution. Mayruhk studied the surrounding area, making sure to check back to where he spotted the figures in the distance. The van was mostly empty aside from the captive, who sat fastened to the side by buckles with dense foam wedged between her body and interior.

"Ms. Jacobs! It's Mayruhk!" Mayruhk shouted as he climbed into the van. "I'ma untie you!" He waited until he finished his announcement and gaped at Etana's continuous fight with her restraints.

Etana jerked her head up, eyes squinted. "Mm mmmmm. Mm mmmmm," she muffled until her eyes seemed to widen with amazement. "Mm," she mumbled before she allowed her neck and mouth to finally relax.

Mayruhk took the opportunity to gently take the duct tape off her mouth. "Thanks," Etana said and relaxed her neck and closed her eyes.

Mayruhk studied the remaining restraints and removed them with caution. Occasionally he would turn to a stiff Josiah, who sat between the large open doors. "Are the rest of your bodyguards gonna come just in case?" Mayruhk asked after a couple of panicked looks towards Josiah's back.

"What other bodyguards?" Etana answered in a calm demeanor.

Mayruhk hesitated on his next statement as his thoughts were drowned in the sounds of sirens. "That's them coming for us?" Mayruhk called as his voice echoed off the metallic walls.

"Yeah," Josiah answered and then continued to watch the approaching lights. He stood up and walked away from the truck.

A heavyset man in uniform slowly approached Josiah with slight shifts in his hips until he stopped. Josiah immediately backed away with an angled-off body. Confused, the officer took a couple more steps only to find that moving closer caused the same effect.

"Woah there," he said, and then reached into his vest and pulled out a small tablet.

Josiah watched every movement the man made. "I can hear you," he said and then added, "You good where you at."

The man chuckled as he tapped on the face of the pad. "I'm sorry, I'm just a bit confused," he said, and then looked Josiah in his eyes. He took a step forward with an outstretched hand. "I'm Detective Matthews."

Silence consumed any want for a conversation as Josiah stood motionless for a second and then placed his right hand in his pocket.

The detective chuckled again, a little more exaggerated than the last. "Okay," he mumbled to himself. "Just so you know, I'm here to help and just want to ask a couple questions about what happened. But I understand you may be startled and not ready to speak yet." His thick accent overtook in a seeming attempt to soothe.

Josiah rolled his eyes and sighed. "Sure."

The detective glared at Josiah for a moment before reviewing the text on his tablet. "Can you describe to me what happened?" he asked with exaggerated movements from his free hand. "Just what you saw and experienced." He tapped the lower half of the screen and held the tablet out a small distance from his chest.

Josiah glanced at the tablet and saw a microphone that flashed in red. "I don't know who they are, but some people came and I'm pretty sure that they just wanted to take, uh... Ms. Jacobs."

"Any reason you can think of that might have caused this?" the detective followed up and checked the screen of the tablet.

Josiah shook his head. "I don't know her like that," he answered, and then observed his surroundings as an officer passed by with a heavy camera in his hands.

"That's fine," the detective said as he followed what Josiah was paying attention to. "Can you tell me your reason for being here?"

"Yeah," Josiah answered and focused on Detective Matthews again. "I'm here for a business trip with my co-worker. Um... we were supposed to get names to help grow businesses in the community and sell and give away some products."

"Okay, and who is the company you work for?" the detective asked.

"Amirnation," Josiah responded, but noticed a small twitch in the detective's eyes.

"Duke Amir." Detective Matthews said, and then looked at Josiah with an irritated look he tried to resist. "How long have you worked for him?"

Josiah stood tall with a cocked head and squinted eyes. "Not long, but I'm sorry what does that have to do with the shooting?"

"Just trying to get as much information as possible," the detective rebutted. "What's your relationship to Ms. Jacobs?"

Josiah hesitated. "I just met her today. She showed us around a bit, and then it happened right after."

"The attempted abduction and shooting, right?" the detective asked.

Josiah paused for a moment again. "Yes," he finally said.

"Can you tell me what happened from your point of view?" the detective asked.

Josiah took a small breath before speaking. "Um... me and my co-worker came here to host at this event for our company. We just got started when some dudes pulled up. At first I thought they were a part of the event, but then they shot the security and tried to take Ms. Jacobs," Josiah explained, and then pointed at Etana while she was being tended to by a medical officer. "And then they tried to get me," Josiah finished with a wipe of his nose.

"Mmm, okay," said the detective. "Is there anything else you'd like to add?" he asked.

"Not right now," Josiah said as the officers studied each section of the crime scene nearest him.

"Okay." the detective said, placing the tablet into his vest again. "I just need to ask your co-worker the same, and you boys will be on your way."

"Mm," Josiah responded, and then looked down at his feet. After the detective walked a short way away, he watched as he interacted with a calm Mayruhk.

They spoke casually, as if it were a daily occurrence. Mayruhk's mouth moved without hesitation after brief pauses in his movement. He then watched as Mayruhk pointed in his direction, which made him concentrate harder on guessing the flow of the conversation.

"Yeah, we came here together," Mayruhk answered, as his arm fell to his side and then behind his back. He looked over once more to see Josiah observing them like a predator in tall grass.

"And from what he told me, you both work for Amirnation under Duke Amir?" the detective asked, and then followed Mayruhk's eyes to see an officer taking pictures with a controlled drone.

"Yessir," Mayruhk answered while changing his target. "As liaisons," he followed up.

"And from your perspective, what happened?" the detective asked.

Mayruhk hesitated for a moment. He studied the van behind the detective and traced a path along the ground. "We were setting up over there," Mayruhk said, and accidentally pointed at Josiah.

\* \* \*

Josiah held the phone tight to his face after hearing the beep through the speaker. He sighed and took a moment as looked to the far corner of the room he adapted to. "Hey, just checking in. I know everyone probably out or at work, but um, sorry for not calling earlier. We wanted to make a good first impression and be there early. At least my partner did." Josiah sniffled a little as he examined the window that framed a part of the quiet neighborhood. "But um, we got in the rental, but I just wanted to make sure everyone was good. I just... I just need to talk to you... about something."

Josiah lowered his phone until it laid face down on the thick orange blanket that covered the unfamiliar mattress. He brushed the bottom portion of his socks against the hardwood floor as he slowly hunched himself and massaged his temple. "Food!" he exclaimed and then pushed himself up toward the direction of the exit. The door was easily swung open before he mindlessly led his body to the right with his phone firmly held a few inches from his chin. Soon, an alarming sound caught his attention and he turned to aim for the stairs leading to the main floor.

"Yo!" Josiah called.

"What's up bro?" Mayruhk replied while laid across the living room couch

"I'm finna cop some food off the app, were you tryna grab something?" Josiah asked as he hovered over the end of the couch where Mayruhk's feet rested.

"Yeah," Mayruhk replied, followed with a couple loud cracks from his toes. "What's open?"

Josiah tossed his phone on Mayruhk's stomach. "The fuck, why would you do that?" Mayruhk asked with a face of pure disgust.

Josiah sucked his teeth. "Come on, son. You'll be 'ight," he snapped back within what sounded like one continuous sentence. "I'm just letting you see what they got and just hit me with answer."

Mayruhk threw the phone back. "I'll take waffles if they have it. If not, I'm okay."

Josiah snickered while he tapped away at his phone screen. "Anything with it?"

"Scrambled eggs and water," Mayruhk shouted and then added, "No cheese."

"I got you," Josiah replied. "You got cash app?"

"Yeah," Mayruhk replied, his attention still captured by the options on the streaming service. Soon the loud thuds from Josiah's heavy steps echoed louder than the TV, and Mayruhk raised the volume while shaking his head.

The motions of animated characters took back his focus. He entertained himself with the harmless actions of each character's interaction until they lost the spotlight. But moments later, it became harder to pay attention to what each character said, and it became more apparent that an ensuing conflict was scripted to start. Mayruhk watched as one character blasted a hole into the other after an exchange of words he couldn't make out. Another flash on the screen, and more characters lost their lives in a dramatic fashion.

Mayruhk pushed himself up to lay on his side. "I'm good."

The channels flickered under Mayruhk's control. He stopped on a police show, but the familiar lights from the police car deterred him from the channel.

Next, he recognized a children's show, and with no hesitation he gave in to the nostalgia. He played with the idea of mental escape as he slowly placed the remote on the side table and returned his attention to the dancing personifications of objects and fantasy characters.

A time-lapse ensued before a lesson was forced upon the viewer in a cheesy manner. They talked heavily about safety and the unpredictability of some events. Mayruhk took a deep breath as he unnecessarily followed along with the message being taught. It didn't take much for him to give into the urge to change topics, and he instantly sat upright and turned off the TV. He slumped over and touched various parts of his face.

"I think the food is here," Josiah shouted, startling Mayruhk in the process. "Can you just check the window real quick? It should be a black sedan!"

Mayruhk turned his head to see an unfamiliar car stationed at the end of the walkway. "Yeah..." Mayruhk said irritated.

"You said the food's here?" Josiah yelled as he sped down the steps, fixing his shirt.

"Yeah, I'm pretty sure that's the car outside," Mayruhk answered as he became more attentive to the conversation and made small gestures to prepare himself to stand up.

"Good looks," Josiah said as he copied Mayruhk's actions to peek out of the window. "I didn't get no call or nothing."

"For real, for real, you should call just in case," Mayruhk said with a look of desperate concern.

Josiah mumbled to himself while reading the text on his phone, and constantly looked out into the night. "Yeah. Yeah," he said with a slightly higher pitch. He then moved to his sneakers and aggressively rammed the heel of his shoe on the floor. "Ight, I'ma head out." Josiah snickered as he left the house, leaving Mayruhk to shake his head until the door slammed.

Mayruhk stared at the door for a moment. Without sound, the room felt empty, and he could feel an unsettling ache in his stomach. He placed his hand firmly over his eyes, and then dragged them down and around the bridge of his nose until only the fingertips covered his eyes. "Mmm," he groaned to himself as he unveiled his eyes, and he instantly started to massage his head while the groaning continued. His feet dragged along the floor until he gained a sudden nerve to stand up, but the sound of the opening door startled him.

"Yo," Josiah called as he swung the door open like a sitcom character. He then took a second to notice a frozen Mayruhk, who seemed to await his next move with wide brown eyes. "My fault, I know we on high alert, but yo... tell me how this mofo just pulled off.

And I know he saw me because son looked dead at me," he said aggressively tapping on his phone's screen.

Mayruhk jerked his neck back. "They didn't call, they just pulled off?"

"My fault, hold up real quick," Josiah said with a face heavily illuminated as he walked to the nearest window and pressed against the glass to see down the block. "Lemme call this dude. Who pulls off and not say anything?"

"For real, for real, he might have the wrong address. That happens," Mayruhk said and pushed himself up to walk over to the window.

"He ain't picking up," Josiah immediately replied, making room for Mayruhk and walking toward the door.

"He stopped up the block, right?"

"Yes, black SUV. Hello?" Josiah asked with the mic of the phone pointed at his lips. "Hello, you passed a whole two houses. Can you back up? Huh?" Josiah paused. His eyes were squinted heavily as he pressed the tilted speaker against his face. "Okay, I got you, but are you able to back up two houses? I'm right here."

"What happened?" Mayruhk asked, concerned as he watched Josiah shove his phone into the pocket of his dark blue denim.

Josiah stared at Mayruhk for a second. A small smirk began to emerge. "I hung up. So hopefully he don't spit in our food, but nah," Josiah said as he swung the door open again. "How I'm telling you,

you drove two houses down, drive back: but we still talking on the phone like... I don't know, be right back," he added as he checked for a response before he studied all angles of the outside and continued into the cool night.

Josiah sped across the lawn while strains of grass leapt off his heels. His attention constantly fell upon his phone as he constantly reviewed the information on the driver and car. As he approached the car, he noticed the windows were heavily tinted, but could vaguely see a human silhouette in the back seat as he passed. He checked his phone, only to be astonished by the position of the delivery car in relation to the blue dot.

"Get in the car," commanded a hushed voice. Josiah turned his head to see a man just below his height with an extended arm, holding an object that reflected the red glow of the rear lights. "Don't turn around."

Josiah immediately threw his hands up by his ears. "You, uh... I ain't... I ain't got no cash, man. Come on son, just be easy, and... and I got a couple other things you can have," Josiah pleaded, and then turned around to face his robber.

"Who the fuck told you to do anything else, coon?" said the man aggressively. He stepped closer to give Josiah a clearer picture of the rabbit hole he may find his destiny in.

"Look man," Josiah cried with a quiver in his speech. He rocked left to right with his hands lowered to his chest. "You can have anything, man. I..."

The man turned his attention to the car, and within a split second, Josiah launched a *nakadaka* fist that landed on the artery of the man's neck as he removed his body from the centerline. A bang rattled him off balance and he collided into the sedan, which made a jerk forward.

Josiah stabilized himself mostly on the side mirror, with his hand firmly pressed to his left ear. But his assailant's movements in agony sparked a fast response that lead to a front kick to his inner knee, followed by a roundhouse knee to the temple.

Soon, the rear door swung open and nearly knocked Josiah over. As the passenger attempted to push past the laid body, he was greeted with rapid kicks that continuously pressed the man's upper body between the door. The man whimpered in pain as the door kept a beat against his arm, until the car was driven forward and knocked Josiah back. It slammed its open door into a parked car as the passenger slipped back inside after a hit to the head. The car backed up and drove off to leave Josiah to recover in a white cloud.

\* \* \*

Minutes earlier, Mayruhk had dropped to the floor in hopes that the sofa would defend him from the gun that just fired. His heart played a beat on the cold wooden floor as he laid frozen in fear of the situation; only the simulations of past movies advised him.

Suddenly, the door was forced open. Mayruhk scrambled back to separate himself a little more from the sound's destination. He listened as multiple heavy footsteps and voices traveled throughout the house.

"Window," he whispered to himself, praying that he was awarded enough time to dive bomb out the living room window and dash to safety as he rehearsed the actions in his mind. He slithered back some more until his eyes could visualize the opportunity that awaited. He slowly moved to his hands and knees as he struggled to position himself into a low running stance. His breathing tightened up as he listened to the footsteps move faster, with added thumping in various areas. But a set of boots seemed to be closer than he anticipated.

"Got him," a man said, walking around the edge of the sofa with a pistol aimed at his target's body. He cocked his head slightly at the sight, and then positioned his weapon to Mayruhk's head. "Already looking for forgiveness?" he asked.

Without pretense, Mayruhk pushed forward, pressing his forearm against the man's inner knee and cupping the back of his ankle with his hand before pulling.

"Fuck!" the assailant shouted as he swung the blunt part of the gun onto Mayruhk's upper trap. Instinctively, Mayruhk grabbed the assailant's arm before the next swing, folded the man's arm over his, and pushed in the opposite direction until his shoulder popped.

"Ahh!" the man shouted as his body jolted under the weight of Mayruhk.

"Freeze!" shouted another from the space that separated the hallway from the living area. He stood relaxed, with his gun pushed forward and held in a solid grip.

Mayruhk rolled to his side and carried the weakened man to use as his personal barrier. He then pressed his soles into the man's chest and thrusted him toward the threat. But his opponent side-stepped behind the wall, letting his partner collapse as his head slammed against the railing. Mayruhk then jumped behind the side of the couch. Kicking his partner's body out of the way, the assailant went to recover his ground, only to be met with objects thrown in his general direction.

"Ya'll couldn't handle that fucking boy!" shouted the third man behind the heavy thumps of his boots.

"Just gimme one good minute," the other replied, itching to get the opportunity to turn the corner.

Without any nearby options, Mayruhk picked up the sofa and pinned it to the walls; mostly closing the entry point for his attackers.

Surprised, the closest man went to kick the barrier down, but to no avail. "The fuck? Help me get this shit down!" he called, pausing for a second to the sound of shattering glass.

"Aw, hell naw!" said the man on the stairs as he rushed down and began shooting the walls and sofa.

Frantically, Mayruhk dropped to the floor as a few bullets and cotton grazed him. He then crawled towards the recently broken window he initially set his goal on.

"Stop that shit!" shouted the other man. "You trying to fuck up the money?!"

"Mayruhk!"

The two men started arguing, giving Mayruhk the opportunity to propel his body through the remains of the window, enduring the pain as he rolled off the cracked screen of the television and into a full sprint.

"Mayruhk!"

Ignoring all obstacles, Mayruhk continued to sprint, making short stops to flag down any neighbors with the words, "Fire!" yelling with spit spewing from his mouth. Soon the sound of heavy strides caught his attention, and he turned around with the intention to grab whoever was moving aggressively toward him. To his surprise, Josiah slipped his outreached arm with a disrespected look on his face.

"Aye yo?" he asked after he slipped past Mayruhk. Josiah quickly grabbed Mayruhk by the arm and directed his movement into the nearby corner store. "Fuck!" Josiah yelled, and slammed his phone to the ground.

"Can I help you?" asked the clerk with widened eyes, studying the intimidating frames of the larger men.

Mayruhk just glanced at the man, ignoring his question while Josiah paced. "This ain't no coincidence!" Josiah mumbled angrily to himself. "How the fuck..." he said with squinted eyes aimed at the ground. He quickly looked at his phone.

"Is something the matter?" the clerk asked, and then stepped back. Without warning, Josiah carried his cracked phone to the exit and threw it past the open glass door. "Excuse me?!" the clerk called, and his hands moved toward the bottom portion of the counter.

"Why'd you do that?" Mayruhk asked, with shifting eyes changing focus from the door to an upset Josiah. "We still have to call the cops and get our ride back home!"

"Nah," Josiah said. "Those dudes came in the car that I called; I can't think of any other way they could've gotten to us," he explained, and then breathed into his clasp hands while his eyes teared up.

"Excuse me!" the clerk said. "But you have to go; if you no buy, you must go," he said firmly, pointing toward the door.

Mayruhk stepped to the counter and mouthed the different item names in the back. "Do you have a phone we can borrow?" he asked and then looked over to his frantic co-worker, who was now watching the street through the stickers on the door. "I just need to call the cops real quick."

"No," the clerk said without hesitation. "You have to go."

Mayruhk threw his hands up. "You don't have a phone at all?" he asked in dismay and searched the bodega quickly. "What if I buy something; then can you call the cops for us?"

"Okay, okay; you buy, I call cops on you," the clerk said.

"For us," Josiah interrupted when Mayruhk hesitated to respond.

"Okay, okay," the clerk said and then reached in his pocket to pull out his phone.

"You still got your wallet on you?" Mayruhk asked with trembling hands.

"Yeah," Josiah said, after he wiped clean his eyes. He reached into his pocket while maintaining vigilance as best he could until he tossed a metal rectangle.

"Hello, yes    I have two men here, and they say they are in need of some assistance  " the clerk said over the phone, and then continued to give requested information. "Yes?" the clerk asked after he placed the phone on the counter.

Mayruhk passed the items, unenthused by the situation. He rolled his neck and caught a glimpse of Josiah crouched down along the windowpane.

"No, please leave," the clerk said, and addressed Josiah with a pointed index.

Without argument, Josiah stood and slowly left the store. Mayruhk followed outside and took a seat next to the slouched body of Josiah. The cool air whistled over the sound of tearing plastic while Mayruhk struggled to balance various loose items on his thighs.

"What the fuck is going on?" Josiah asked from beneath the cover of his folded arms. He looked up and cautiously took a large hat offered by Mayruhk. "Thanks," he said, and placed the hat loosely on the front-most part of his head to cover his face.

"I don't know," Mayruhk mumbled, and kept a constant onlook past the small parking lot from under a shirt draped over his head. "I don't know."

Josiah peeked over at his co-worker like a turtle in its shell. He noticed Mayruhk's unease as his head stayed on a constant swivel. After slight admiration, he propped himself up and assisted with watching the block. "We gon' make it out," Josiah said, and nodded his head. He then placed his hand on Mayruhk's back, which startled him, and gave small rubs on his rear deltoid muscle. "Yeah..." he added, and then kept to himself for a moment before burrowing his head again.

Mayruhk continued to stare off into the distance with random jerks from his neck when a car would pass. "Do you believe those stories when people can do things ...like lift cars off people?"

Josiah made slight adjustments in his position. "I never thought about it," Josiah answered. "But I ain't gon' hold you, my dad told me about stuff like that."

Mayruhk remained quiet after Josiah's answer. Soon the sound of police sirens echoed in the distance "Were they true?"

"I believed them," Josiah responded and followed with clearing his throat. "I think it has to do with the release of endorphins that allow you to focus more...I can't think straight though."

Mayruhk's mouth opened to form his next statement, but was drowned out by the fast moving cars that turned into the parking lot.

Their blinding red and blue lights danced upon the white canvas that covered his head until he removed it to reveal his face.

* * *

Mayruhk studied the bright lights in front of him with a consistent distraction from the men and women dressed in blue. The heaviness from his eyelids slowly made it hard for him to concentrate in the armchair he slouched in, but he kept picking a fight with the laws of human nature. "Bro!" Mayruhk called as a policewoman carried a cup of water toward their general direction. He lazily pressed the point of his elbow into the side on the arm supporting Josiah's head.

Josiah looked up to the face of the uniformed woman while she stood over him patiently. He studied the cup firmly grasped between her rose-colored nails. "Thank you," he whispered and placed the water on the ground.

"Don't mention it," she said and took a seat at the desk beside them. "If what was discovered last night in Red Bank what you two described it; I'm not surprised he keeps falling asleep. But I know you want to call your employer and rush out of here, and if you still feel like you'll be okay until you leave today, you just let me know, okay?" she explained, leaning forward with her hand elegantly placed under her chin.

"Okay," Josiah responded.

"Yes, Ma'am," Mayruhk added.

"Okay, there you go," she said and passed them a wireless phone.

A few seconds later, Duke answered the other line. "Good morning," he said.

"Hey... Mr. Amir. This is Josiah Williams. We had like two shootings that happened while we were here," Josiah explained, rubbing his forehead. "Can you send us a plane to leave today; this afternoon if possible?" he asked, and took a deep breath as he waited for the response.

"You were shot at?" Duke yelled, followed by the background noise of scrambling and shouting. "Hold on; I'm handling things right now."

Josiah looked over at Mayruhk, who was struggling to stay conscious. "Yo," he said, nudging Mayruhk. "We about to be out soon."

"Josiah!" Duke called.

"Yes," Josiah responded. "I'm here."

"Okay, here's what I need you to do," Duke began. "Have you accepted any protection from the police station you're at?"

Josiah propped himself up and attempted to focus himself. "Not yet, but I can. How long will it take to get a plane here?" he asked with rising concern.

"No, don't," Duke replied, sparking a reaction of confusion from Josiah. "What you're going to do is meet Ms. Jacobs."

"Why?" Josiah asked with a slightly higher pitch.

"She'll have a better explanation, but as of right now, she's your best bet for gaining an understanding and protection," Duke explained.

"Ms. Jacobs knows why they came for us?" Josiah asked, and then looked and turned away from the intrigued eyes of the officer.

"Yes," Duke answered. "In that city, she has a high level of control over what's going on. She's a very influential character, and although it may not seem like it, she will have information on what's happening and whether it's safe to leave."

"Why can't we just get on the plane and go home before anything else happens?" Josiah asked with a staggered breath in reaction to the unfortunate news.

"I'd rather not set you up in an open position," Duke explained. "If you're telling me you were assaulted twice... the first I'm assuming happened at the festival. I just saw that this morning; but I'm going to assume you were there early, too, and they just threw you in with 'others' on the report. But the second time, I didn't know about until now. So, if they went for you two separate times, I would not give them a third."

Josiah took a deep breath. "What if... what if I asked for protection until we leave?"

"You could," Duke said. "But, with the rumored history and known history of that area... I'd like you to trust me, and prepare yourself, so you know what, when, how, and why; and then we will move from there."

"Okay," Josiah said, and peered over to check on his co-worker. "So, what do we do? Walk?" Josiah asked while checking around the station.

"No," Duke answered. "I'll put things in motion. An officer will gather you and you will go from there. I will have more information about your flight later today."

Josiah took a strong breath through his nose and felt the beating in his chest. "All right," he said.

"All right, see you soon," Duke said, and then hung up.

"Thank you," Josiah said.

"I got these two," Detective Matthews said. "Well, look what we got here."

\* \* \*

The scenery was immaculate. Many people of multi-shades of brown walked through the clean streets of the neighborhood, dressed in high-quality fashion. The police car didn't seem to amuse them as kids swerved around the front on bicycles like a top gun pilot. Men watered the trees and spoke like gentlemen when passed by a familiar face. The sun danced on the windows of businesses as they passed, but the backdrop of various items and clothing could not be ignored despite the performance. On one of the taller buildings amongst the ones among the strip mall, a mural stating, *Proud to be black-owned!*

featured a curly haired woman who appeared to be screaming the words at the top of her lungs.

"Hmm," Mayruhk said.

Yeah, it's a nice place," said Detective Matthews after peeking at the rearview mirror. "It started in 1964, if I'm not mistaken, but it's gone through so many terrorist attacks it's hard to tell. The idea held strong, though, and that's what you're seeing now."

"Mmmm," the two men said almost at once.

"Yeah... to tell ya the truth, I'm actually hoping people take up after this place," he said, and then leaned forward to turn the car. "We have a lot of pride here, and it's comfortable, but what I like the most is that given the history of this town, Ms. Jacobs was able to turn it around and protect this place. I mean, it's terrible what happened yesterday, but that only shows she's doing things right by us to have the white man that mad again."

"Mmmm..." Mayruhk responded, now intrigued by the dialogue.

"Is this why we're going to her?" Josiah asked and then mumbled, "Because she can protect a town."

"Well, it's a lot more than that, but you know, you will get to chop it up with her soon enough and really get to learn what makes her such a threat."

\* \* \*

The fancy door swung open, and Etana stood in plain view. Water ran down her forehead like streams from underneath her towel. "Oooh, I know why you're here," she said, and then stepped behind the door. She soon created a sweeping motion with her hand until the young men took the hint.

The door slammed behind them, and a heavy aroma of floral scents rushed past Mayruhk and Josiah immediately after the shock from the loud noise. They watched as Etana led the way, aggressively rubbing the vanilla cloth between her hands and head. "Um..." Mayruhk began, briefly motionless, until Josiah followed with unquestioned trust. He squinted as he watched his co-worker walk until he disappeared into the other room. After a shake of his head, he traced their steps into a small living space with no pronounced décor except for a framed collection of scribbles and a smart television.

"I'm sorry for putting you in a situation like that yesterday," Etana said sincerely, and then covered the upper part of her white crew neck with her towel. Wet curls draped over her face while she sat on the gray set piece and pulled a comb from her sweatpants pocket. "The couch is still free," she said, pointing with the head of the wide-toothed comb.

"Can you tell us what happened, and why we had people finding us?" Josiah asked with fury in his eyes. "Is it because of you?"

Etana smirked and then paused her session to face the hardwood floors. "Yes, and no," she admitted.

"So, just because we were there... wait, who are these people, and has this happened to anybody else?" Josiah asked, flooding the conversation with his curiosity and then rushing to the end of the sofa nearest to Etana.

"It didn't follow all that," she said, looking up. "But an explanation—well, my explanation—is all I can offer."

"Ight," Josiah said, looking to Mayruhk with no exchange.

Etana sat back with perked lips and began combing along the grain. "Given the history of this city, let's just say the ideals and fairness amongst the people here ain't too great. Just to keep a long story short. But some time ago, 'bout a couple years back, Duke and I assisted a group that continuously fought to bring equality for our people, but peacefully." She paused for a moment, and then placed the comb on one of the armrests. "But after a certain point, some of us grew tired of the constant cycle of us doing something nice and harmless, just to be met with an attack or blatant disrespect. But Duke and I at least saw eye to eye on one thing; we both knew how to fight, defend, be independent." She nodded her head as she finished the sentence.

Mayruhk and Josiah followed her hand as she waved her hand in a circle. "That's where this came from," she explained and then reclaimed the comb. "We fought for this continuously, but that's where your problem comes in. When the majority feels the need to hold power despite what they admit to being true, they hate it when you fight, and I know you've seen or at least heard the things that happen even when all you do is talk—or even nothing, for that matter."

"We just got here," Josiah argued. "What's that gotta do with us?"

Etana paused her actions and stared at Josiah with perked lips and squinted eyes.

"It's because we work for Duke," Mayruhk mumbled, watching as Etana rolled her eyes twice toward Mayruhk's. "And they threw our ass in the same boat."

"And what do you mean, 'what this got to do with ya'?" Etana asked, darting her eyes at Josiah. "You don't see what ya look like?"

"That's not what I meant," Josiah argued and then leaned back.

"What did Duke do, though?" Mayruhk asked as an immediate follow up.

Etana laughed. "We fought anyone that tried to tear this place down, and whoever tried to come for one of us. But we really caught a fixin' from this biker gang called the Angels of Wrath; the same men that attacked us yesterday," she answered, and then continued. "A short time ago, they added trafficking black kids to their catalogue amongst other things, and we've been fucking them up for the most part. But I made it worse by hosting an event that partially was going to promote more self-defense and protective measures for our communities."

"Why don't they just mind they fucking business and leave us alone?" Josiah exclaimed with a twisted look on his face. He pressed his hands down towards his knees with a deep inhale and release. "I just wanted to do my job, have fun, and go home."

"I'm so sorry, sweetheart," Etana said with sincerity and rubbed his shoulder momentarily. "Unfortunately, black bodies are a high commodity. It's weird, and I understand that depending where you go, our value changes. But here, the Angels do what they can to profit, and fortunately we stand so much in the way, they had to personally come to try and get me out of the game. With a punk-ass surprise attack, too."

Mayruhk studied Etana's behavior as she began to calmly comb her hair again. He attempted to speak, but instead locked eyes with her. She gave him a gentle smile. "Don't worry. They may be able to surprise us in a public park, but we hold most of the control here."

"What can we do, then?" Mayruhk asked.

Etana propped herself up. "Okay, here's the plan," Etana began, and then cleared her throat. "A plane was sent for your departure, but we're gonna go about it my way, given our current situation. The plane will be here at 6:30 a.m., so you two will be there at the airport early."

"Are you coming with us?" Mayruhk interrupted.

"No," Etana responded. "Also, I'm speaking," she said with her hand placed on her upper chest, and then continued. "I predict something may happen, so in the chance that something does, I have some preparing to do."

Josiah and Mayruhk sat attentive for the remainder of Etana's speech. "You're gonna wait there. One of you will take the upper deck, and the other the lower. This time, in case anything does happen, you two have a better advantage. At the very best, you can hop on the plane and carry on outta here."

"So, you just want us to wait until something happens?" Josiah asked, disturbed by the notion.

"Hopefully," Etana said. "But if not, there's one more thing I need you to do."

They leaned in as she prepared herself to discuss the next part of her plan. "Most likely, being that the Angels appear when not wanted, I anticipate they'll try to do something to prevent you boys from leaving to hurt the company, or maybe just to get at Duke himself. Anywho, one of the issues is that people and officials in this city tend to turn a blind eye when they abduct members of our community or market the incident for a moment. I ain't asking much, but I want you to record what you see, just to build a moral case against them."

"How is recording going to help, and what happens if they come for us again?" Josiah asked with excitement.

Etana paused for a moment. "Ah well, I ain't gunna suga coat, so, I don't trust this country's leaders or care for them, and I know they don't care too much for me either, and that's nice. But what I'ma do is set countermeasures. If they want to play dumb, especially when it comes to my city, my people—well then, I'ma make sure to keep track of every stupid thing so I can show my friends and make some new ones."

"You want evidence to keep for yourself?" Mayruhk asked with a raised brow.

"Yes," Etana answered with no time to breath. "And not for blackmail; just to sometimes add to the cause and get a better effect." She pointed her index at Mayruhk.

"Mm, okay."

"Anywho, I want two vantage points covered. Mayruhk on the top floor as guidance, since you're always in your thoughts, and Josiah on the main floor as the enforcer, since you seem to act first and question later."

"Wait, what?" they both asked around the same time.

"It shouldn't be hard, but this will give us proof of the Angels' attacks on the black community, and possibly capture some police involvement based on what they've done in the past."

"No, what am I enforcing?" Josiah asked frantically.

"Hopefully, nothing," Etana replied. "But when push comes to shove, you will have to fight. I really don't want you too involved or even around, but unfortunately you don't get to choose. That's not my choice, but until things are better; I gave you my best strategy with what we have."

"But we only been to the terminal once..." Mayruhk argued.

"That's why you're going early," Etana responded. "You get time to prepare, plus I'ma have y'all hooked up with equipment. Nothing like the movies, but y'all always be able to hear from me at... almost any given time."

Mayruhk checked his phone after seeing the shock on Josiah's face. "Are your bodyguards going to be there?" Mayruhk asked with a sudden burst of energy. "The, the, the ones that did the shooting?"

"Sure, Mayruhk," Etana said with a playful smile.

"What?" Mayruhk asked with a face like he smelled something spoiled.

\* \* \*

"How are things going, Mayruhk?" Etana asked, her voice clear as it traveled through the earpiece.

"I still have eyes on them," Mayruhk admitted as he focused the phone's camera as close as possible on the three police cars parked on the runway. He turned the camera to the tall man standing calmly at the top of the plane steps. The man spoke with diplomacy as he attempted to stop the officers from advancing forward, but his action bore no fruition.

"They're taking him in now," Mayruhk answered. He recorded the officer aggressively handling the pilot's lanky frame as he stumbled to hold proper footing. "In cuffs," he added.

"Got it," Josiah answered in a hush tone. He kept his body pressed against the wall, peering through a door held slightly ajar. "They in?" he asked nervously.

"Yeah... I got you, bro." Mayruhk said. "I'm going to count down when they get close, but you can leave now."

On cue, Josiah exited the dark room quietly and left the door open. He looked to the northwest to find his co-worker crouched against the railing of the upper balcony. With a slight head nod for confidence, he walked quickly through the corridor toward the front of the building.

"They're about to be on your left turning the corner. One on each side of the pilot; similar height on both men." Mayruhk took a deep breath as he monitored each party moving at a moderate pace toward each other. "All right, I'ma count down—remember, one on each side and our dude in the middle."

"Copy," Josiah said quickly with a slight tremble in his voice.

"Five, four..." Mayruhk began listening to Josiah inhale and exhale with controlled breaths.

Josiah followed along with the timing of Mayruhk's counting as he neared the corner. The rising sun reflected off the metal strip that covered the edge of the corner, but the glare soon passed as Josiah swung his body to the right. The last few digits rang clear in his ear, and soon enough, the brim of one of the officer's hats peeked around the corner. Without hesitation, Josiah swung his body with his leg dragging behind until it rose high in the air.

The sound of a heavy smack echoed down the hall as Josiah's foot collided with the nearest officer's face. As the man flew backward, Josiah positioned himself to jump above the head of the pilot. He muscled through, angling his body to deliver a hook kick to the back of the surprised receiver, but noticed that the pilot had crouched midway through his motions. After he landed, he watched with a dropped jaw as the pilot kicked the officer as he attempted to recover.

"Josiah!" Mayruhk shouted, and drew Josiah's attention to the recovering officer whose hand was itching for his pistol. Josiah immediately pressed forward, and push-kicked through the officer's knee. He then followed with an elbow to the temple while the man yelled in agony.

"Shit," Mayruhk said, still focused on Josiah and the pilot. He peered outside and watched the demeanor of the other officers change slowly after hearing the amplified sound from the terminal. "Y'all might have to start moving, and I'll keep track of them until I gotta run."

"Keep going to the plane, Mayruhk," Etana said through the earpiece. "Stop!" she shouted, forcing the remaining officers to freeze in position with some drawing their weapons and others simply placing their hand to the handle. They watched as five SUVs drove up and formed a semi-circle facing the unwanted party. Etana quickly stepped out of an already open passenger door and walked to the front with an automatic rested comfortably in her arms. Other men and woman peered from behind the doors of each vehicle with some positioned at the rear, carrying various weapons.

"I knew you'd poke your head around here sometime," one of the officers said as his voice grew louder in the earpiece. Mayruhk continued to watch as the remaining law men shuffled into a semi-circle as one of them stood confident against Etana's group.

"That's nice!" she replied, then she shrugged her shoulders. "I don't see how that's gonna do ya any good, but I'm guessing that if you claim to like using that brain of yours, you'd want to keep it."

The officer stared at Etana without any audibles. "Mayruhk, let's go!" Josiah's voice rang through the earpiece, which motivated Mayruhk to move with the camera and continue downstairs.

"You see, I don't agree with what you got going on, and what makes it worse is that those boys don't got nothing to do with Duke's decisions," Etana's voice carried over the earpiece.

"Your argument falls short when they work for him," the officer said. "And now you can't argue that!"

"How you went after them ain't right," she rebutted while shaking her head. "But you see, we're gonna make it right. Those boys are getting on that plane," she said, reinforcing her grip on the gun.

Mayruhk listened as sounds of clicks and inaudible noises echoed through the mic. Mayruhk paused for a moment to look out over the clear panels shortly after arriving at the first floor. "Y'all Angels lost a lot messing around with me. I don't think it's wise to take a couple more Ls," Etana said over the calming commotion.

"Then you gon' rot for striking down an officer of the law," the officer said. "A white officer, at that."

"The crazy thing is, after years of this back and forth crap, do you really believe I'll carry on without gathering some type of hard proof?" she sucked her teeth in disappointment. "Come on, now; I'm a little bit smarter than to let you say some Oscar-nominating lines like that and not let the world see it."

Mayruhk watched as the officers frantically observed their surroundings, until someone pointed in the direction of Josiah and the pilot striding toward the plane. Instantly, Mayruhk observed the signs and sprinted after his co-worker. "Also, we know good and well that the reason y'all are here is bullshit; what are you going to say, anonymous tip of possible drugs?" Etana looked away in disgust and then continued. "Take the L, and if you're lucky, you'll probably get to harass me from your porch again like them good ol' days."

Mayruhk watched as the two head figures interacted as if he was being subjected to a real-life drama. "Mayruhk, where you at?!" Josiah yelled over the mic with such concern that it snapped Mayruhk back into reality.

Mayruhk turned back one more time and manipulated the camera lens to zoom in on the individual license plates from his better angle on the main floor to outside. Attention quickly shifted to Mayruhk when both groups turned to watch the man now stationed with a phone at his chest level. He resembled a noisy child who had just been discovered by his mother's group of friends at a late party. He looked at Etana for direction, but she kept her focus mostly on the man she had argued with.

But, for a small instant, she locked eyes with Mayruhk, and gave him a nod with an added finger motion mimicking a push broom. "I'm coming up now," he answered, and then sprinted up the steps.

"You got everything?" Josiah asked with a tremble in his voice.

* * *

Duke examined the phone on his desk as a video played. He tapped the screen and noted it was nearing the end. With a few finger movements, he returned the size of the video to message form where Mayruhk's name was listed at the top of the screen. "Yes, I got everything," he responded to Josiah's question and then stared at his phone. Duke took a deep breath. A soft click finally disturbed the silence. "Over the years... the nature of my service has changed. My overall goal, everything, became... *intertwined,* for lack of a better word, with the problems targeting people of our community. Not that I or we as a company dealt with individual issues, but things of a macro-political and social nature, and some economic imbalances." Duke rubbed his grizzly chin. "After a while, I gained a lot of unwanted attention. No different from when a celebrity gets the attention of assaults on their craft, as well as physical; you know what I mean," Duke finished with slight nods while his chin rested on caressing fingers.

"What did you do in Chattanooga?" Josiah asked. "Tell us everything."

"I can't explain everything, but I can give you a few things," Duke answered immediately.

"Include what was so bad that a whole biker gang was coming after us off the strength of your name," Mayruhk demanded.

Duke hesitated for a moment and leaned back calmly. "Well, why my name or company probably brought so much attention is because of my position as a leader in this country. Not to brag, but I'm a big dude that speaks well on how he feels, openly. To make it worse, I have money, knowledge, support, and no allegiance or care for a good majority of European practices or figures in place against me. With all that, I go from being born as a major threat in European society to a person that needs to be disposed of..."

Mayruhk squinted in response to the statement.

"So, people want to murder you because you're a black leader?" Josiah said without a moment of quiet. "Like all black leaders get murdered. What did you do specifically in Chattanooga?"

"Well, no, and I'd like to believe there is more to it than that," Duke began. "The host of public events to add to the community, teaching self-defense, the well-built neighborhood; I committed a lot to ensure the success of those things and more. But this is still a country that targets our race for the most trivial things. Yes, what I said is very vague, because it has applied in every state; but depending on where you land, it ignites different responses. What probably puts me on the chopping block is my network... it would take most of the country's network to take mine down. Most importantly, I've made it difficult to murder anyone within my circle; I've taken a lot of control over our population," Duke finished, and watched the expressions change on his employees' faces.

Josiah raised a brow and then briefly turned away with a smack of his tongue.

Duke slightly opened his mouth but hesitated to release any words. "My network and ability to make dramatic changes within the black community?" Duke asked with a tilt of his head and squinted eyes.

"'Ight," Josiah conceded. "You got it."

Duke sighed. "You weren't meant to be dragged into this. It was planned for you to be my representatives until my return, that is all," Duke said passionately.

"Well, somehow... not somehow, because they came for us. They plotted and made moves on us as if we always had beef." Mayruhk shrugged his shoulders. "Why go so hard? And... and that's not even it. All of it. Because you had people, and your people knew what was up."

"Fucking... fucking pilot had to know," Josiah intervened. "Had to... too calm, and not on some instructions you gave him the day of, because apparently no one knew this was gonna happen."

Mayruhk took intense breaths and stared off for a moment forcefully batting his eyelashes.

"You weren't expected to have to witness that," Duke answered, and then nodded his head.

"No, yeah, he didn't panic or nothing; just beat a man and walk off... and then fly a plane, naw fam."

"Well, yeah." Duke hesitated. "But I made sure he was trained to combat these issues."

"What?" Josiah turned to Mayruhk and then back to Duke. "And you didn't think that someone would associate us with you? So, everyone else seems to know what's up. But you sent us in blind!"

"No, it's because you're not me," Duke replied. "I didn't immediately expect this kind of reaction to people the public barely knows. I could understand if I mentored you, but as far as the public knows, you started last week, and they may think of the interview."

"Maybe it's because we're the weakest link, and killing us makes it easier to get to you," Mayruhk argued.

"I understand where you are coming from, but publicly, the company is separate from my personal actions, and no one else has experienced this reaction. You're not the only ones here," Duke argued as his character showed signs of breakage, but he shortly returned to his mellow persona.

"It doesn't matter! It doesn't matter!" Mayruhk struggled to form his sentence. "They see you, or something they believe is you, and they're coming."

"I understand, but this group has not attacked others that work for me," Duke argued. "But since that seems to be a concern of yours...

hang on," he finished as he raised his phone off the desk and quickly placed it back down after a few taps with his thumb.

Josiah sneered at Duke as time elapsed; his easy-going attitude wasn't attractive. Duke turned away and ignored the ugly face Josiah made. "Anyway, to answer your next concern. You were always protected, despite the illusion you were on your own. Now, I didn't explain to you every aspect that came with working with me, but I still kept the unlikely in the back of my mind. A 'prepare for the worst, expect the best' attitude."

Shortly after Duke ended his response, he looked toward the door and smiled. The sound of heavy boots echoed off the walls of the room and stole the audience. A dark-skinned woman about average American height walked by Mayruhk without a noticeable change in attitude as the men gaped at her movements. She stood beside Duke, fitted in a black turtleneck combined with rugged tactical pants that hugged her exaggerated hourglass figure, this laid under a custom dark green technical jacket that draped over her developed shoulders and abdominal muscles.

"I assume you've been wondering who I am?" She looked at them unenthused and soon began to tap her boot beneath the power of her large leg. "For a while now, I can guess. You can call me Hazel."

"Why did you say you were a bodyguard for?" Mayruhk asked briefly after her introduction. "Couldn't you have helped us all?!"

"I did support you... well, we did." Hazel replied. "I'm sorry for what happened, but I'm not meant to be a gun you get to wave at your leisure."

Mayruhk glared at Duke and then back at Hazel. "So, you just follow us around... what happens if we don't do what you want?" he asked as his hands began to shake while gripping the armrest.

"No, but maybe I came off as if I had bad intentions."

"She's not to blame. I took the liberty as a leader looking to protect his circle, but with the pretense that nothing would happen—not to startle you, but keeping in mind the reality of being a powerful African descendant in America. That's why I had designated guards over you," Duke intervened and usurped Hazel. "You're two young black men with knowledge of how to harm others, and currently represent a company known for supporting and uplifting African descendants of many professions and allowing them to walk down avenues safely with little opposition from individuals in this country. Unfortunately, that's your image, depending on who paints the picture."

"Why did you choose us?" Josiah asked, his head slightly bowed and pupils angled off to the corner beneath lazy eyelids. "I want to believe you have good intentions, so please..." His weary eyes searched for the attraction to his question. "That's the only thing ringing in my head right now."

Duke gasped softly. "What I envision when I look at you both are the embodiments of similar universal energy as the sun and moon. I place my trust in the universe, and believe in matching the energies of certain organisms. So, that being said, I cosign with the idea that in this universe we can attract things to ourselves and also emit energy or vibrations that effect other beings. Josiah, you have a more direct approach to things and allow beings to grow in your presence through your burning desires. Like a strong magnetic pull, you invite people in despite how you feel. Mayruhk, you're more reserved and cautious about how you reveal yourself, and adapt yourself to almost any situation. You still emit a radiance that's just as intoxicating as the sun, but a smaller percentage will see it. And that's fine; I just view you as more discreet, calculated, and precise when selecting your goals and company," Duke explained.

"We emit energy like the sun and moon?" Josiah questioned while Mayruhk kept his eyes strained.

"Theoretically," Duke answered. "What I'm proposing is that people like you have an easier time navigating through life despite the bumps which everyone experiences. You can influence the environment in a way that what you deem true will most likely happen, almost like being clairvoyant."

Mayruhk scrunched his face. "And you knew this from looks?"

"From a couple of reasons."

"Like?"

"Your attitude about things, what you've talked to me about, as well as your public profiles, referrals, how you react to things..." Duke answered quickly. "But most importantly, how you were able to manipulate the universe in order to attract what you wanted or needed accomplished."

"Hm," Mayruhk grunted. "Because we're more... *capable*... of accomplishing certain things?"

"I didn't drag you into anything," Duke snapped back. "What happened was unexpected, and yeah, I'm sorry for getting you involved, but whatever happened didn't involve my cooperation, and if it did, why would I go out the way to bring you back to bust me about something I did? Things happen *all—the—time*, but we plan to counter them. I understand my name carries weight, but some of that weight is unknown, unjustified, and I do not assist in planning attacks on my own... especially not in my company."

Josiah stared at the man, shaking his head in small movements. "Nah... I don't know," he said, and took a heavy-chested breath. "I damn sure don't know, man."

"We have to think about it," Mayruhk stated and then looked over to a confused Josiah.

Duke raised an eyebrow. "I see," he replied. "Josiah?"

Josiah hesitated for a moment with eyes that wandered the ground. "Yeah, I need some time to think," he replied with eyes that interlocked with Duke's. "And thank you for that; I can speak for myself."

"Last thing, though." Mayruhk scratched his bare cheek, then transitioned to the back of his head. "Are you proactive about this, and how? And can we see what you have done for handling situations that may come?"

Duke grinned, leaning gracefully into the plush leather back. "Of course. It would go against my character. But long story short, whomever is involved will be trained in advanced combat that complements the abilities of the individual or individuals. We are also implementing... actually, you know what—stop by tomorrow, I'll send you a synopsis of what I plan to do and how. Also, we can discuss any concerns and then do a little showcase, because I want to show you the bioware..." Duke halted on his racetrack of words as if crashing into a wall after moving a thousand miles per hour. "Tomorrow. We will meet."

"How are we getting it?" Mayruhk questioned.

"I have physical copies here, or if you like I can email you," Duke replied.

"I'll take both," Mayruhk answered with a brief look toward Josiah, who asked for only the email at the same time.

"Understood!" Duke said, leaning over slightly to open and close a drawer within his desk. "Here," he said as he handed Mayruhk a thick black folder sandwiching yellow sheets.

Mayruhk accepted the gift and then immediately gathered his belongings.

"Not going to look it over?" Duke asked.

"I'll check it when I get to my apartment," he replied, and then exited after only a single glance toward Josiah, who was checking his phone as he stood.

"Hmm," Duke mumbled to himself as he and his associates witnessed the back of Josiah's blazer disappearing behind the organized array of red, green, and black.

"They're not coming back," the woman stated before she turned to face Duke. "You could've had trained professionals, and I will keep saying that until it sticks. You could have manipulated or molded them the same way if anything changed a couple things, but I don't think they are built for this."

Duke nodded his head. "You're right in a sense—in terms of militant tactics, but this isn't something so... you know, restrictive... to only that aspect."

"It may not be the same status as a war, but once guns are drawn, it's a battlefield, and a military-style leader may be better. Now, I get that this was one group of some street gang, but one time is good enough for me to expect something similar again," she said in a calm but stern demeanor. She glanced over to the door and stepped in closer. "We need to be moving tighter than we were before, and having poorly trained kids fight for us ain't it... it ain't it."

"What if I had something else to throw in?" Duke asked.

"I'ma find a counter, but what?" she argued.

Duke inhaled deeply, slowly raising his hand in a limp posture before making a 'c' motion in the air. "I'm looking for specifics, not a well-rounded person. I need specific strengths and weaknesses. Abilities and resources to overpower our enemies, but not just force." Duke chuckled and then slightly turned away, noticing no change in the recipient's attitude. "But most importantly, I don't want someone so influenced by the manipulators of this land that they turn to political correctness to justify their actions. Plus, in terms of the law of attraction, they have a great chance of invoking what I want to achieve and maintain."

The woman hesitated with her response. "I'll be back," she finally replied with a puzzled look on her face. "They're still kids... young, and should have different guidance when it comes to shit like this. I don't give a fuck if they can fight or have a high survival rate."

Duke smirked. "You guide my blind eyes. Thank you," he said as he looked up at her. In that instance, she placed the blank mask over her face once again. "I'm taking the half hour to study... plan stuff if anyone asks; I won't be answering." His command was adhered without conflict before Duke was left alone to stare off for a moment. Soon, he began to tap with haste on his keyboard. The room slowly transformed into a darker accommodation, and a white screen revealed itself from its hidden slot that blended into the vanilla sky.

"Yes?" a woman asked as the screen loaded, and Duke moved to place an earpiece in one ear.

Etana's still image soon filled the white blanket briefly before she revealed herself, looking off in the distance as the camera captured the underside of her face. The position soon changed as she panned past her thick lips and high cheekbones to create a more frontal profile. "You gon' speak?"

Duke chuckled gently. "So... about this weekend," he finally said.

Made in United States
North Haven, CT
08 November 2021

10960550R00059